"I missed being here." His eyes searched hers. "And I missed seeing you."

The temperature rose. Her cheeks burned as she gazed at him, not knowing if she should say thank-you or toss out a lighthearted comment. Before she could move, he slipped his arm around her.

"What's Brandon up to now?"

The change in topic caught her off guard. "Resting. No school until next week, but he's fine."

"I'm relieved." He brushed her cheek with his index finger.

His eyes searched hers, making her uncomfortable. She didn't understand the touch or his embrace. Her mind spun. "Did you see the living room?"

His head jerked back as if she'd surprised him. "No. I came in through the garage."

She struggled for breath. "Come take a look." She beckoned to him, trying to keep her hands from shaking. She needed to get a grip.

He followed her lead, and when he reached the archway, he stopped, his gaze sweeping the room. "Wow! That makes a difference."

"Do you like it?"

"I do, but..."

She hung on his voice, waiting for him to finish the sentence, but he only gazed at her. "But what?"

Quinn drew closer and slipped both arms around her. "But I like you more."

Books by Gail Gaymer Martin

Love Inspired

*Loving Treasures
*Loving Hearts
Easter Blessings
  "The Butterfly Garden"
The Harvest
  "All Good Gifts"
*Loving Ways
*Loving Care
Adam's Promise
*Loving Promises
*Loving Feelings
*Loving Tenderness
†In His Eyes
†With Christmas in His Heart
†In His Dreams
†Family in His Heart

Dad in Training
Groom in Training
Bride in Training
**A Dad of His Own
**A Family of Their Own
Christmas Gifts
  "Small Town Christmas"
**A Dream of His Own

Steeple Hill Books

The Christmas Kite
Finding Christmas
That Christmas Feeling
  "Christmas Moon"

*Loving
†Michigan Islands
**Dreams Come True

GAIL GAYMER MARTIN

A former counselor and educator, Gail Gaymer Martin is an award-winning author, writing women's fiction, romance and romantic suspense. This is her forty-seventh published novel, and she has over three million books in print. Gail is the author of twenty-eight worship resource books and *Writing the Christian Romance* released by Writer's Digest Books. She is a cofounder of American Christian Fiction Writers, a member of the ACFW Great Lakes Chapter and a member of the Faith, Hope & Love Chapter of RWA.

When not writing, Gail enjoys traveling, speaking at churches and libraries, presenting writing workshops across the country and singing as a soloist, praise leader and choir member at her church, where she plays handbells and hand chimes, as well. Gail also sings with one of the finest Christian chorales in Michigan, the Detroit Lutheran Singers. Gail is a lifelong resident of Michigan and lives with her husband, Bob, in the Detroit suburbs. Visit her website at www.gailmartin.com. Write to Gail at P.O. Box 760063, Lathrup Village, MI 48076, or at authorgailmartin@aol.com. She enjoys hearing from readers.

A Dream of His Own

Gail Gaymer Martin

Love Inspired

Recycling programs
for this product may
not exist in your area.

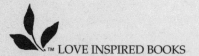

™ LOVE INSPIRED BOOKS

ISBN-13: 978-0-373-87746-1

A DREAM OF HIS OWN

Copyright © 2012 by Gail Gaymer Martin

www.LoveInspiredBooks.com

Printed in U.S.A.

Do not store up for yourselves treasures on earth,
where moth and rust destroy,
and where thieves break in and steal.
But store up for yourselves treasures in heaven.
—*Matthew* 6:19, 20

Thanks to my Facebook group,
Readers of Gail Gaymer Martin's Books,
for their support, ideas and amazing comments and reviews. Without readers, an author's books would sit on shelves. Thanks to the Michigan Secretary of State for providing detailed information on the process for obtaining a driver's license. Today the rules are very different from my day. Thanks also to Wendy at B&B Collision for answering my many questions about accident repairs. And always, my deepest thanks go to my husband, Bob. Without his support and love, I wouldn't be the writer I am today.

Chapter One

Quinn O'Neill shifted in reverse as he checked his rear and side view mirrors at ACO Hardware. He lifted his foot from the brake and inched backward from the parking spot, his mind filled with the numerous repairs needed to return his home to what it must have looked like ninety years ago when it was new. Too bad repairing himself wasn't as easy, but money wouldn't fix him.

Quinn's thoughts were interrupted by a thud, and a crunch of metal jarred his SUV. He slammed on the brake and jammed the gear into Park, then bolted outside eyeing a car embedded in his back quarter panel, the shiny black paint gouged and buckled against the woman's dark red sedan.

She glared at him from the driver's window, her eyes narrowed as determination set in her jaw. She pushed open her car door with a dramatic sweep, stepped out and slammed it. "Look what you've done." Her arm swung toward the damage. Shattered glass from the taillight dotted the asphalt, and her trunk lid had sprung loose from the lock.

Trying to monitor his frustration, he shook his head. "It wasn't my fault. I checked my mirrors." He peered back at her. "More than once." Yet in the back of his mind, he knew he'd been distracted by his thoughts. Could he have been careless?

She bustled closer. "Do you think I don't check my mirrors?"

"I have no idea, but—" Seeing tears collecting in her eyes, he felt less inclined to argue. "Are you okay?" He skimmed her frame, noticing beyond her distraught expression how attractive she was.

Her eyes snapped from him to her sedan. "I'm fine, but I can't be without a car, and if I report the accident, my insurance rates will go up. I can't afford—" Words rushed from her like air from a pricked balloon. Once she recovered, she waved her hand in the air. "Never mind. It's not your problem." She paled and pressed her hand to her heart, her fingernails painted the color of a ripe peach.

He eyed her hand. No wedding band, and probably a one-car family. Ice slid through his veins. He didn't allow himself to make mistakes. Not when it came to driving. He pulled out his wallet for his insurance information. "We should call the police."

Panic struck her face. "Police? For what? They don't care about fender-denters."

Despite her alarmed expression, he chuckled. "You mean fender-benders."

She evaded his eyes. "Whatever."

"I suppose. The police have enough to do. Neither of us is injured."

She gave a decisive nod and strode closer to her damaged sedan. When she tried to force down the trunk lid, it resisted.

"Let me help." He moved past her and forced it downward, but it refused to catch. He eyed his quarter panel damage. It fared better than her sedan. "I might have something in my car to tie it down."

When he lifted his trunk lid, a horn tooted. He gave the guy a shrug as he pointed to the damage. The man made an obscene gesture before he backed up and moved off. Quinn shook his head. What happened to kindness and compassion?

After scouring inside his trunk for a piece of rope, anything to secure the lid, he found nothing. Discouraged, he straightened. "You didn't happen to purchase something in the hardware store we could use, did you? String? Twine? Tape?"

She shook her head. "No. Only O-rings, gaskets, washers, pipe joint compound and a wrench."

Plumbing supplies. His brow tugged upward, his curiosity spiked. What did she know about O-rings?

She leaned into her trunk and came up shaking her head. Moisture hinted in her eyes. "I'll run inside and buy—"

His chest constricted. "Let me." As he opened his wallet to pull out some bills, a blue strand beneath his backseat caught his eye. He reached in and drew out a bungee cord. He held it up. "No need. This will work."

Though she'd accepted his help, the woman remained cautious and hadn't given him the hint of a grin even though she'd made him chuckle. Still he'd spotted her smile lines traveling from her full cheeks to her well-shaped lips, the same color as her fingernails. He'd love to see her smile and to ask about the plumbing supplies. Instead, he focused on the situation, winding the cord around the bumper and through the inside workings of the trunk until he secured the lid. "I'll follow you to a body shop."

"A body shop?" She closed her eyes, the strain evident on her face. "I have no idea where one is." She shook her head. "I'll…I'll drive home and call a friend." She glanced at her watch. "Lexie should be home."

Quinn's jaw slacked, hearing the uncommon name. "Lexie Fox?"

She drew back, her eyes widening. "Do you know her?"

"She and Ethan are members of my church."

Her eyes glazed as if unable to comprehend what he'd said. "Really?"

"Really."

She gazed at him without a response, her face taut.

He rubbed his hands together, sensing he had to do something to relieve her stress. "I'm here. There's a body shop a few blocks from here on Main Street. Randy will give you a free estimate."

"Free?"

"No charge."

Her eyes narrowed. "Why are you doing this?"

Something about her tugged at his heart as he managed to grin. "I'm a nice guy."

Her suspect expression melted. "I guess you are."

Quinn had to look away to stop his pulse from racing. "It's on my way home." He eyed his SUV's damage, his heart sinking. "I'll follow you to keep an eye on your trunk. If it pops up, pull over."

Her shoulders lifted in a sigh. "Thanks." She rotated her wrist and looked at her watch. "I'll be late getting home. I should call my son."

A son. Blurred memories raced through his mind.

She delved into her handbag, pulled out a cell phone and pressed a couple of buttons.

Though he stepped back, her voice reached him.

"Bran. This is Mom." She pressed her lips together as she listened. "You want to what?" The corners of her mouth pulled down. "Okay, but be home by eight. No later and no excuses."

Quinn's lungs constricted as the boy's baritone voice murmured from her cell phone so like his son's.

"No. I'm running a little late. I didn't want you to worry." She paused as if ready to disconnect. Instead she pulled the phone back to her ear. "Did you take your pills?" She nodded.

"Good. Now remember. Eight o'clock. And no excuses, Brandon." She clicked off and slipped the phone into her handbag.

Quinn waited, a multitude of questions rattling in his head—questions about her son, about the medication and about her and the hint of tears.

She looked into the distance and said nothing.

Silence pressed against his ears. He'd lived with silence and had accepted it as a way of life, but this was different. He wanted to know her.

"Why do problems always come in a row?" Her voice caught him off guard, and when he looked at her, her eyes said far more than her words.

"I don't know." His guilt-riddled thoughts intensified as he reviewed checking his mirrors. Since the tragic accident, he'd become overly cautious. But had he been today? "Problems multiply." His certainly had.

As if the wind had been knocked out of her, she nodded. "My son is bugging me about his learner's permit. He's completing his classes, and every day he asks and whines about why I'm not enthusiastic. Once he starts driving, my insurance will…" Her brows furrowed.

He suspected she'd picked up on his distraction. He struggled to dig himself from the deep crevice. "Teens can be persistent."

His feeble response hung in the air as he diverted the conversation by giving her directions to the body shop. In the driver's seat, he pulled forward to give her room to back out while the sound of grating metal assaulted his ears.

She maneuvered the sedan into the lane and drove ahead, her trunk lid bouncing with each bump in the road.

When they reached Main Street, she followed his instructions and turned left. Quinn eyed her short brown hair glinting in the sunlight through the rear window. He had to admit she was attractive with skin like cream, not one blemish, and intense hazel eyes. He liked her independence. She didn't jump at his offer to help. She'd considered it first, eyeing him with suspicion. She'd been smart to question his motives and probably questioned why a stranger would offer to help.

She'd given evidence of being a single mom. The burden of decisions about her son's driving, the cost of insurance and even a trip to the hardware seemed to rest on her shoulders. He tried to picture her doing her own plumbing. Her feminine frame looked sturdy enough to handle a wrench, but her manicured nails and slender arms didn't fit any plumber he'd seen. Then again, not wearing a wedding band didn't negate being married. But why not call a plumber? That's what he did.

Quinn's thoughts snapped back to the situation at hand. He concentrated so much on her trunk lid he'd forgotten the damage to his own vehicle. He needed an estimate, too. The who-was-at-fault issue dug deep in his mind, but seeing her financial concern and the difficulty of being without a car, he wondered if he should take the blame. It was an accident.

Without warning, the word cut to his heart. Accidents should never happen. Everyone knew that. They were excuses for carelessness and for...

Quinn grappled with his frustration, Frustration meant defeat, and he was done with that. He clamped his jaw, his grip tight on the steering wheel as if the action could control his indecision.

A red light caught him unaware, and he jammed his foot on the brake, thanking the Lord he didn't hit the back of the woman's car again. The woman? He cringed. They hadn't even exchanged names or information. His preoccupation had gotten the best of him.

The light turned green, and he drove through the intersection. Ahead, he could see the B & B Collision sign. She saw it, too, since she hit her right signal. He slowed and stopped behind the sedan, waiting for traffic to clear.

* * *

Ava could see the man through her rearview mirror. His mouth was locked tight. He would be a prime example of why she'd hesitated to add fathers to the Mothers of Special Kids support group, but the women had voted to let them join anyway.

At the newly named Parents of Special Kids organization, she'd branded herself the inquisitor. She wanted to view all sides of an issue, and often she served as the devil's advocate. Not everyone liked that, she knew. And now that men were part of POSK, she'd realized she'd been wrong about most men's unwillingness to talk about their problems, but not incorrect about this man. She'd never met one so closed off.

Something in his introspective eyes had ignited her inquisitive nature, yet she didn't know him well enough to pry. Didn't know him at all, in fact. They hadn't introduced themselves, and she should have asked for insurance information. The accident was his fault she was certain. Or quite certain. She'd checked her mirrors.

Ava wondered if the man realized he didn't know her name. Maybe she could be as closed-mouthed as he was and remain a nameless woman. He apparently liked to be in control, but he'd met his match today. Ava Darnell wasn't easy to push around. She sighed, dismissing her ridiculous thoughts.

His knowing Lexie and Ethan had eased her mind, but she'd been distracted by his good looks. The streaks of gray contrasting with his wavy dark hair had raised an age question, but studying his features, she suspected he wasn't too far from her almost thirty-nine years. And he'd looked at her with those eyes—gorgeous eyes, blue ones that seemed to search her soul. Or was he searching his own? She may never learn a thing about him. But two could play the silent game.

Traffic cleared and Ava veered into the parking lot with

the SUV following behind her. A body shop made her miserable. She didn't have the money to deal with a damaged car. Making ends meet was enough of a challenge, especially with her steep mortgage. With the mention of her house payment, her thoughts flew to the financial mess Tom had left behind.

She gazed at the shop door and cringed. What did she know about cars and repairs? Yet seeing the nameless man slip from his SUV, her confidence lifted as he approached her. She spun around with false assurance and headed for the entrance.

Before she reached the door, he dashed ahead of her and held it open. She headed for the counter. So did he.

From the garage, the sound of a static-filled radio station was punctuated with clanks of metal and intermittent thuds. A man glanced in from the garage and held up his index finger, and in moments, he charged through the doorway, wiping his hands on a dirty rag. "Quinn, what are you doing here?"

Quinn. She gave a sidelong look at the man beside her. Irish name. He looked Irish—the dark Irish with the amazing blue eyes and raven hair. He reached forward and grasped the man's hand with a shake, and then nodded toward her. She wanted to give her own nod toward him. He'd caused the accident.

Quinn preceded to tell the story, chuckling as he called it a fender-denter, directing another nod her way.

Finally she gave her own nod. "He backed out of the parking spot into me." She put a little emphasis on the *he* and *me*, hoping the man Quinn had called Randy got the point.

Randy gave him a flickering grin before looking at her with an unsuccessful attempt to appear serious. "So you both need an estimate."

She pushed her way closer to the counter. "Yes, it's my trunk lid. It has a dent and now the lid won't lock."

He pulled out a form and grabbed a pencil. "Name?"

So much for being nameless. "Ava Darnell." As she spoke, she dug into her bag and pulled her driver's license from her wallet, then slid it on the counter.

He glanced at it. "Phone number?"

She eyed Quinn, but he was looking at her license. She wanted to cover it with her hand. "You won't need my number. We're going to wait."

"You're welcome to wait." He tilted his head, his pencil poised. "But I still need your phone number."

She drew up her shoulders and gave him her number.

He pulled out another form and jotted Quinn's name at the top. She couldn't read the last name, and Quinn spieled off his telephone number. The area code was local, but she expected that.

"I know you have insurance, Quinn." He turned to her. "How about you, Ms. Darnell?"

She reached for her wallet again. "I have insurance." Her stomach churned knowing she'd still have a deductible. Where would she get the money?

"No." Quinn's voice startled her.

Randy scowled, his eyes shifting from her to Quinn. "Which is it?"

"I have insurance." She delved into her bag.

"The accident was my fault."

Quinn's admission stopped her cold. "You admit it?"

Quinn ignored her and looked at Randy. "I'd prefer to pay for whatever she needs. Pretend she doesn't have insurance."

His meddling heightened her irritation. She attempted to save money, but she wasn't a pauper if that's what he thought. "Please, I have—"

His eyes captured hers. "I know, but allow me to do this."

Addled, she slipped the strap of her bag onto her shoulder and studied him.

Randy dropped the pencil on the counter. "Whatever you say." He pointed to the garage. "I have a job to finish. It'll take another twenty minutes or so. You can wait here if you want. I'll get to your cars as soon as I can." He motioned to the chairs in the waiting area.

Ava strode across the room, sank into a seat and closed her eyes. When she opened them, Quinn stood beside her. She scrutinized him a moment. "What's wrong with you?"

He drew back, his eyes widening. "What?" He shook his head and looked away. "I'm trying to be conscientious."

"I have insurance."

He sank beside her. "And a deductible." His head lowered as if he were looking for a further response on the floor.

Though the deductible was correct, Ava still didn't understand his determination to pay. "I have a job." The income wasn't great, but it was a job. "I don't need charity."

He lifted his head, his expression darkened by her judgment. "I know you aren't looking for a handout, and I'm sorry it came across the wrong way."

Her teeth clamped over the inside of her bottom lip, and she wished she'd kept her mouth shut. "I'm sorry. I—" She straightened her shoulders. "We haven't been introduced properly. I'm Ava Darnell." She extended her hand as much for goodwill as for her introduction.

Quinn peered at it a second before grasping it. "Quinn O'Neill."

Definitely Irish. She gave his hand a firm shake. "Let's hear the estimate before you make offers, okay?"

Though his eyes darkened, he nodded and leaned forward, resting his elbows on his knees. He seemed to find the floor interesting.

She settled into silence, trying to understand this man. His offer to pay for her repairs seemed odd, but it took all kinds of people to make up the world. Maybe he was a staunch Christian compelled to show kindness or generosity. Whatever it was, she hoped he wasn't a scam artist. She flinched, realizing her attitude stemmed from her late husband Tom's financial problems. She had to be more trusting. He said he knew Lexie and Ethan. Still, being a single woman always put the fear of being ripped off in the forefront of her mind.

Quinn watched Ava in his peripheral vision. Her determination to resist his help drove him crazy. On the other hand, he admired her, too—her pride and her self-assurance. He couldn't help but notice how she'd charged from her car after she'd parked outside. She walked with a decisive manner, her head high and her solid frame giving her an air of knowing what she was doing.

Lydia had a way of carrying herself that showed her confidence and her receptiveness. That's what had attracted him when he met her. She'd made a perfect wife for him, the owner of a prestigious business. She knew how to plan excellent dinner parties and how to add elegance to even the simplest event. He couldn't imagine meeting another woman like Lydia, and yet today those attributes weren't as important as they had been. After her death, he'd readjusted his priorities. His old life had been self-centered, more driven to earn status and wealth. Now other things were more important.

When Ava shifted in the chair, her knee bumped his. He lifted his gaze to her face, aware she had something on her mind.

"It's difficult being a single parent."

One of his questions had been answered. She was single as he suspected. "How old is your son?"

"He turned fifteen a few weeks ago."

His lungs drained of air. His son had been fifteen when he died—full of life, strong and ready to tackle the world and often his father. The trait had grinded Quinn, and his own determination grew to show Sean who was boss. He'd done it the day Sean and Lydia died in the horrendous car crash when a drunk driver hit them head-on.

The day burst into his mind. Tired of jumping to Sean's

every whim, he'd said no to his nagging about taking him out to practice driving. The new learner's permit burned in Sean's hand. Despite his son's insistence, he'd refused, but Lydia determined if he wouldn't take Sean for a driving lesson, she would. He didn't stop her. The old ache knifed his chest. If he'd given in and gone with Sean that day, the accident may have been avoided. He would have been quicker to grab the wheel than Lydia. She rarely drove.

His lawyer insisted on suing, and they'd won, but the money meant nothing to him. It couldn't buy back his wife and son. It couldn't fill his empty heart. It couldn't replace everything that was precious. That's when he realized that his business, his wealth, his success meant nothing at all. He'd cursed God. A God who promised to be faithful. A God who assured His children He heard their prayers. For so long those empty promises controlled his life. But time healed even the deepest wound, and he'd made restitution with the Lord, clawing his way up from darkness into the light of faith. He would never have survived without it.

Quinn's thoughts cleared, and he noticed Ava looking at him. How long had he been silent? "Fifteen. They can be difficult at that age."

She studied him a moment as if curious about his silence. "You must have experience with teens."

Her comment tore into his heart, and he couldn't speak.

But it didn't seem to matter. For her, talking seemed more urgent. "Teens get to a certain age, and they think they know everything. I'm sure you've experienced that?"

"Teens are teens." He didn't want to encourage the line of conversation. As Ava studied him, his skin crawled.

Then she fell silent for a moment. But after taking a lengthy breath, she turned to him again. "Brandon has Hodgkin's lymphoma."

A knife ripped him again. Though he wanted to say something kind or wise, he couldn't find the words.

Yet her voice brightened. "But he's in remission. I'm so grateful."

She waited for his response, but he still couldn't go there. His own loss weighted his mind. Finally he managed a "that's great." But not wanting to continue the conversation, he did the next best thing. He tried to lighten his tone. "So you purchased washers, O-rings and a wrench at the hardware." It wasn't exactly a question, but he wanted an answer.

"Of all things, my kitchen faucet leaks." She offered a fleeting grin that sent his pulse skittering. "I plan to fix it myself."

His heart rate escalated as her smile lines deepened. "You'll fix it?" Grateful for the new topic, his mind wrapped around a dimple flickering in her cheek. He tried to picture her repairing the leak. His only involvement in repairing a faucet had consisted of paying the plumber.

Her brows lifted. "I read articles on how to do plumbing repairs on the internet. It's not hard, and it saves money."

Hearing her reference awakened his regret. He had more money than he needed. She had to tighten her finances while dealing with a seriously ill son. Her courage amazed him.

Quinn studied her profile, his gaze lingering on her ear decorated with a small jeweled earring, the stone the color of a leaf budding in spring. She wore her hair short but with a slight wave curving at her neck. On the left side, she tucked the strands behind her ear.

As his thoughts sank in, Quinn cringed and glanced away. He needed to get a grip. Why would he feel so much concern for a woman he'd only met an hour ago? His emotional reaction irritated him. Yet unable to control his thoughts, he let his gaze drift back to Ava. Proud, strong and capable seemed a good description. A grin played on his lips. He could never picture Lydia shopping at a hardware store and fixing a faucet.

Her eyebrow arched as if she'd noticed his half grin. "You think women can't do plumbing?"

He was the one who couldn't. "No. I think some women can do anything they set their mind to."

"You have more faith in me than I have, but I'm going to do my best."

His stomach churned as he witnessed her brave admission. "I'm only a novice, but could I help?"

Her head jerked upward with question.

"Maybe I could give you a hand…that is, if you run into problems." Air streamed from his lungs as he faced the dumbest suggestion he'd ever made. What did he know about plumbing? He shrank into a chair. "I'll give you my phone number, and you can give me a call." And he could contact a plumber. His shoulders relaxed.

"Thanks. You're too kind."

"Ms. Darnell?"

Quinn's attention shot to the doorway.

Randy strode forward. "I'll need your car keys."

She grasped her handbag and dug out a small ring of keys. "Here you are."

When she dropped them into his hand, Randy turned to him. "I might as well take yours, too."

Quinn pulled the keys from his pocket, and Randy vanished through the garage doorway with the sets of keys as Quinn sank back into the chair wishing he had a magazine or anything that would stop him from offering to do plumbing and feeling his pulse skip each time Ava looked at him. He stretched his legs in front of him, folding his arms over his chest and closing his eyes. Maybe if he concentrated he could get a grip on his wayward emotions. Sean and the accident surged in his mind and was only distracted by the image of the attractive woman beside him, saddled with too many problems.

He remained silent, trying to ignore the waves of Ava's

presence. When she shifted in the chair, her arm brushed his and the hairs on his arms rose. His eyes jerked open. "Sorry about the long wait."

"It's not your fault." She shrugged. "I wish I'd brought in the magazine I picked up at the hardware store. It's on home decor."

Quinn pictured the outside of his once lovely home that needed trim work, and the inside rooms as drab and colorless just as his life had been.

"I love decorating. That would have been a great career for me." The comment sounded as if she was speaking to herself.

His mind ticked with ideas while his heart stretched beyond his belief. He was drawn to this woman in a strange and unexpected way—somewhere between esteem and curiosity. She was different and admirable.

He opened his mouth to speak, but she'd sunk into thought again, and if he allowed it, he'd never learn more about her. "Why didn't you pursue a career in home decorating?"

She turned her head and looked out the window with a shrug. "I married young. My husband had a good job and preferred my staying home."

"So that ended your dream."

Her head swivelled toward him. "I put my energy into my home. I made it my own little showplace."

Pride rose on her face, and he realized she hadn't appreciated his comment. "That's a good use of talent."

Her expression changed. "Thank you, but then you haven't seen my home." Her tone softened. "It's a little worse for wear without the income…the time to keep it up, but I do my best. Most things fall on my shoulders at home. I'm a widow. My husband died a few years ago—five years actually—when Brandon was ten." She drifted away for a moment. "Coronary thrombosis right before my eyes. I asked him if he'd like a cup of coffee, and he said yes. Before I turned my back, he was gone."

Quinn's lungs emptied. "That must have been awful." He had forced the words from his throat. Sean's and Lydia's death had been as swift, but he hadn't witnessed it. Two police officers had come to his door with the horrible news.

"It was a shock." Her voice infiltrated his thoughts. "Tom was young. Only thirty-four. He never knew about Brandon's illness. He'd been gone two years before Bran was diagnosed."

Quinn shook his head. He was forty-five. He couldn't imagine his life ending eleven years early. Sean slipped into his thoughts again. At fifteen his life had ended.

They both sank into silence, and he pondered what to do to make life better for Ava.

Randy reappeared and stepped to the counter. "Damage could have been worse." He bent over the counter and wrote notes on the quote form he'd filled in earlier with their information.

Ava rose first and grasped the form he handed her before Quinn could get a look at the quote. She gazed at it, her eyes losing their color. She pulled out her wallet and slid him her insurance information. "I'll need to use my insurance."

Quinn shifted beside her. "I thought we were going to talk about it."

"No need to talk." She folded the form and slipped it in her purse. "How long will it take to repair?"

Randy glanced at the calendar and then through the garage door as if sizing up the jobs they had. "Maybe three days. Two if we're lucky. If you want, you can bring it in Monday. But you'll need to call your insurance company because they may want you to get another estimate."

Her head jerked toward Quinn and then back to Randy. "Why?"

"It's policy. And if you need a loaner car, I'll call you when one's available. I only have three."

Her downcast look constricted Quinn's chest. "Give us a

minute." He linked his arm in Ava's and pulled her across the room. "I accepted the blame for this, and I want to pay for the damage. Let me see the estimate."

"It's too much." She didn't budge.

"Please, let me decide."

She inched her hand into her purse and pulled out the yellow paper. He opened it and shook his head. The amount meant nothing to him and so much to her and it would affect her insurance rates. "I'll cover this. And forget the insurance company. You don't need the hassle."

Confusion churned in her face. "But why? It's too much money. Why would you do this for me?"

He held the estimate firmly in his grip and searched her face. "Because I can."

Her cheek quivered as tears brimmed her eyes. "I don't accept charity. I told you that, but for some reason, I think this is as important to you as it is to me. So thank you."

Quinn stepped backward, stunned by her awareness. She had read his heart, and it frightened him. Where was he being led and by whom?

Chapter Two

Lexie came through the doorway into the meeting room of Parents of Special Kids at the Royal Oak Senior Center and strode to where Ava was sitting. "You're here. Where's your car?"

Ava shifted her eyes to see if others heard. "I have a loaner."

Lexie sank into the seat beside her. "What happened to your car?"

"I had a little accident."

Lexie eyes widened. "Were you hurt?"

Today Lexie asked probing questions, and it made Ava understand how irritating that could be. She didn't want to talk about her dumb accident. "No. I'm fine." She thought of Lexie's son and grasped the opportunity to change the subject. "How's Cooper?"

"He's doing well. We're so grateful." Lexie gestured toward the parking lot. "So give me details."

Ava gave up. "It was stupid. I was leaving the hardware store, and as I was backing up, we hit each other."

"You backed into a car?" A grin washed away her concern.

Her voice reverberated through the room, and Ava was grateful only a few people overheard. She glanced toward the small group of women. "It was nothing." She waved her right hand and chuckled.

They studied her a moment and then continued their conversation. Keeping her voice soft, Ava told Lexie what happened. Why let everyone else know she'd been careless?

"Was it a guy?"

His image appeared in her mind as a stream of air huffed through her nose. "Quinn O'Neill."

Lexie drew back. "I know him."

"He told me, and to set the record straight, he backed into me."

She eased forward. "Really."

Ava provided her with all the details except that he paid for her repairs. That upset her even more as she thought about it. Lexie's "you backed into a car?" comment made an impact. Her car had hit the side of Quinn's SUV, not the other way around, and she'd let him pay for her damages. More than a thousand dollars. She shouldn't have allowed him to pay. She hadn't even offered him a proper thank-you, and now she felt beholden. She pictured his telephone number still on the back of the hardware receipt where he'd jotted it down.

Lexie eased back when she'd finished. "I'm surprised he knew our names. Quinn sort of sticks to himself. I only know his name, because he helped with some computer issues, and I happened to be in the church office that day working on a mailing. We were introduced."

"You think he's unsociable?" Ava hadn't picked up on that. She'd deducted he wouldn't accept no for an answer.

"Not unsociable really, but on Sunday he's in and out of church. I don't think I've ever seen him stay for coffee hour after the service."

"With me, he was quiet but very kind." And had piqued her interest whether she liked it or not.

"Time to begin." Shirley Jackmeyer's voice rose above the hum of private conversations.

Ava leaned against the chair, relieved that she didn't have to continue the conversation. She hadn't stopped thinking of Quinn since she'd said goodbye at the body shop. Was it his generosity? Or was it unanswered questions? Warmth spread through her as the truth became clear. An unexpected attraction had drawn her to the man, but a man would only complicate her life. Even a friendship wouldn't work.

The chair rattled, drawing her back from her thoughts. Kelsey and Ross Salburg slipped into the chairs beside her. Ava gave them a smile, still amazed to see that a number of faithful men had joined the organization after the women voted to become POSK, a parents' organization. Ross had initiated the change with his desire to be part of the support group.

"Today before we do our sharing, Ross Salburg would like to say a word." Shirley beckoned to him.

Ross rose and strode to the front. As always, his smile brightened the room. "Ethan Fox couldn't be here today, and his wife, Lexie—" he swung his arm toward her "—suggested I deliver his news about the Dreams Come True Foundation. So here I am."

Titters scattered the room.

"Ethan and I were talking about our kids. All of them doing well, by the way." Rousing applause halted his presentation. "Thanks." He gave a nod. "Anyway, Ethan asked me to remind you of the opportunity you have to bring one of your children's wishes to life at no cost to you. Our kids have suffered with their illnesses a long time, and this organization offers them a very special experience. A dream trip for the whole family. Meeting one of your child's favorite heroes. Even something as simple as spending the day with a fireman and riding in the fire truck. The anonymous donor of these funds recently added a healthy contribution so we want to let others in the community know about this great opportunity. Please spread the word. This fund is available to the special kids in all of South Oakland County."

"Ross?"

His head snapped to the right. "Maggie?"

"Is this foundation really from a single donor?"

Ava chuckled. She knew the answer.

"Yes. One person." Ross sent a grin to his wife, Kelsey.

Maggie raised her hand again. "Do we know who it is?"

Ava sputtered at the question. She, too, had been insistent on knowing who it was, but the secret remained. Ethan Fox would be the logical person to know all the details since he represented the Dreams Come True Foundation, but he denied knowing and remained mum.

Ross reiterated the details of the donor for the sake of the newer members, but not knowing the name of the donor still drew everyone's curiosity as it did hers. Members often speculated. She'd done it herself. The reason why the donor remained anonymous was always her next unspoken question.

While Ross returned to his seat, Kelsey leaned over and asked Ava about her car. Her red sedan must stick out in the crowd of cars outside, because she didn't expect both of her friends to notice it was missing. She whispered minimal details about the accident and when the meeting concluded, Kelsey had already told Ross. Both stood beside her asking a multitude of questions. She chuckled to herself. If they kept being so insistent, they would certainly steal her "inquisitor" title.

Kelsey gave Ross a poke. "Was the guy nice?"

The memory rushed over her. "Yes. Very."

"Good-looking?"

The sensation turned to heat. "I'd say so." She could say more, but they would only pry with more questions.

Ross grinned. "Did you get his name? His phone number?"

Emotions rattled her as their toying looks made her

aware of their thoughts. "Quinn O'Neill, and yes, I have his number." It burned in her handbag.

"Quinn O'Neill?"

She didn't like Ross's expression. "What's wrong with him? He goes to Lexie's church."

He shook his head and chuckled. "Nothing as far as I know, and it's Kelsey's and my church, too. I just thought it was a coincidence that he called yesterday about looking at some work he needed done on his home. He lives in an English Tudor not far from the zoo. I think the street is York."

Ava's interest piqued. An English Tudor. She loved those gorgeous houses with turrets and all kinds of interesting rooms. An English Tudor would be easy to spot. One of these days, she might take a ride that way.

Her pulse skipped. What in the world had she become? A stalker.

Quinn checked his watch and noted he had time before his appointment with the contractor. His mind had been on Ava, and he'd hoped she would call about the plumbing, but she hadn't. He wondered if Randy had given her a loaner. He plopped into his desk chair and hit his keyboard spacebar. The monitor came to life, and he typed "white pages" into the search engine and pulled up the page. His fingers poised over the keys, questioning his motive. Then he swallowed and typed Ava Darnell, Royal Oak, Michigan into the search bar. He clicked the cursor, and her name appeared on Blair in Royal Oak—not only her address and phone number but a detailed map to her house. He studied the details, grabbed a pencil and jotted down the information.

When he leaned back and looked at the notepad, his jaw tightened as he tried to comprehend what he was doing. Since the accident, he relived the sound of crunching metal and the thud. He thanked God the accident had been a simple fender-bender. Fender-denter. Ava's phrase made him smile.

Her face hung in his thoughts, and the emotions troubled him. Ava heightened his senses. She made his blood course with her insistent questions. She'd whetted his interest. With her, he felt alive rather than embedded in the past as he'd been for the past few years. On top of it all, she was attractive, not model-beautiful but very appealing. Quinn pictured her full lips curving into a fleeting smile and her eyes twinkling with curiosity when she talked. Ava demonstrated pride, and he admired that. He'd upset her with the insurance issue, and she'd finally allowed him to redeem himself.

In addition, he'd offered to help with the plumbing, but again paying a plumber took no effort on his part. He thought it would be a nice way to make life a little easier for her. She had a sick son. The knowledge humbled him. How would he have reacted if Sean had been diagnosed with a horrible disease? How would he have coped if Sean had lived through the accident and had become paralyzed or brain-damaged or...? Ava's strength awed him.

Quinn pushed himself away from the computer and rose. His head pounded with what-ifs. What if he'd taken time to convince Sean he'd let him practice driving later? What if he'd demanded that Lydia not take him on the road? What if he'd agreed to take Sean for the driving lesson?

The questions had assaulted him since the day the police came to his door. The same responses billowed in his mind. If he'd been in the car, his quick action might have saved his son. He had more experience driving. How many times had he veered away from a near-accident by some thoughtless driver wanting to pass on a dangerous stretch of highway. Life was far more precious than saving a few minutes by being reckless.

He stood in his home office and shook his head. *Let it go. Let it go.* No thoughts or what-ifs could change what had happened. He knew his wife's wishes. Lydia wanted him to live fully. She'd supported him in every way—his preferences, his career and his dreams. She would want him to move on with his life. Instead he'd run away. He'd sold his tremendous home too filled with memories, left his day-to-day business in his brother's hands and moved across Michigan to this small town where he was unknown and bought this house.

As Quinn scanned the room, he admitted it needed paint. He'd meant to fix the place when he'd moved in. Instead he'd blended into the beige walls, had run his company from long distance and sank into regret. No more. Change meant moving ahead, and that's what he wanted to do.

Having purpose for once, he turned off the computer, stepped into the hallway and headed for the kitchen. The late April weather decided to play a trick on spring. A chill clung to the air. He filled the coffeemaker and snapped the on button. In moments, the pungent scent filled the room. As he reached into the cabinet for a cup, the doorbell rang. Quinn veered around and headed for the door.

Ross Salburg, with his sturdy frame and smiling brown eyes, stood on his porch. Quinn greeted him, then stepped back, allowing him to enter. At that moment, he realized Ross's visit was the first in many months. His last visitor had been an electrician he'd hired to upgrade his fuse box. He'd kept to himself, a box locked tight and covered in cobwebs. Pitiful. He shuddered.

Ross scanned the foyer, his eyes shifting to the staircase rising to the second story. "Nice." He ambled to the dining room, gave a nod of approval, and then strode across the foyer and gazed into the living room. "Nice Adam's fireplace."

"I don't use it." The admission darkened his attempt to lighten his mood.

"No?" Ross turned to face him. "This was…is a lovely home."

"That's the operative word—*was*. I've let things get out of hand. When I bought the place three years ago, I planned to update a few things. Now I've let things get shoddy."

A frown slipped to Ross's face, and he turned a full circle, then took a step forward, peering past the staircase to the family room beyond. "You live here alone?"

An ache rose in Quinn's chest. "Yes."

"This is a lot of space for one person." Ross grimaced. "Sorry. I didn't mean to imply—"

"Don't apologize, You're right. It's more room than I need." Quinn envisioned the first-floor master bedroom with its double walk-in closets, roomy bath and vaulted ceiling. He figured most women would love it. "A five-bedroom house is wasted on me."

"Never a waste. You don't know your future. One day you may share it with someone."

Quinn eyed Ross. The man had echoed his own recent thoughts. "I made some coffee." He flagged him toward the family room. "Would you like a cup while we talk?"

"Sounds great. I'll take it black." Ross tucked his hand into one pocket and carried his clipboard in the other as he followed Quinn past the staircase. He faltered in the family room, typical of a contractor who appreciated quality architecture.

Quinn veered into the kitchen, and in a few moments, Ross followed. Quinn motioned him toward the table as he rounded the counter to the coffeemaker. After filling the cups, he headed back to the table, well-lighted by the bay window. He enjoyed his morning coffee there, better than anywhere else in the house. The birds played outside flitting between the trees and the birdbath centered in what should have been a flower garden. The only things that grew now were a few straggly perennials that still had life in them.

He set a cup in front of Ross and then sat across from him. Since he'd called the construction company, he'd wrestled with why he'd contacted it and what he wanted them to do. For so long life seemed empty, almost hopeless, but a renewed urge had appeared egging him to make a difference in his life and in his home.

"Okay, then." Ross took a sip and set down his cup. "You mentioned wanting vinyl trim."

"Right, and new windows throughout. And I'd like an honest opinion regarding the roof shingles. I think they're original."

"Any leaks?" Ross bent over his clipboard taking notes.

"None that I've seen." Quinn's focus shifted to the interior. "I'd like the rooms painted, but I'm not sure about colors. I'll have to give it some thought." His mind flew to Ava who'd mentioned she loved to decorate homes. "I might like a decorator to give me some color ideas. I have no eye for color." He pictured Lydia bringing home paint and fabric samples.

"We can arrange that." He lifted his cup again and took a drink. "By the way, I heard last Tuesday you had a run-in with Ava Darnell." Ross chuckled.

Quinn squirmed. "Right."

"Ava's a nice lady." Ross tapped the pencil against the clipboard. "She's had some real trials. I suppose that's why she was distracted."

"She mentioned her son has Hodgkin's."

Ross nodded. "It's been up and down for her."

"Ava told me she enjoyed home decorating…" Quinn didn't know how to phrase the question.

"Kelsey mentioned how attractive her home is." Ross swung his arm wide. "Nothing like this place though."

Quinn nodded, his mind running rings around his growing apprehension. The size of a home was insignificant. The important thing was the love inside. His thought triggered questions. If that were so what difference did it make what color his rooms were? He wanted them clean, that's all. And making contact with Ava might not be his best move. He should forget her. Forget he even thought about giving her a call.

Ross took a final swig of the coffee and slid back the

chair. "I'll go outside and take a look at your trim, and I'll send someone over to check the shingles. We can talk colors when I bring over some samples."

"Sounds good." But trim colors and shingles didn't linger in his thoughts. Ava's image hung there instead. Options? Did he really have options when it came to her? She'd worked her way into his mind from the moment he saw her.

"Mom. What are you doing?"

Ava's head snapped up from beneath the kitchen cabinet and bonked against a pipe. She grimaced at the pain, lowered the wrench and rubbed the spot with her left hand.

Brandon's face loomed in front of the cabinet door. "You're not trying to do plumbing, are you?" His face registered disbelief.

Surprised at his reaction, she bristled. Who did he think did all the repairs around the house? She ducked out from under the twist of pipes. "I repaired the light switch and the doorbell." Although what she thought would be an easy job hadn't been.

A frown wrinkled Brandon's face. "But plumbing? That's always hard. If you mess with one thing something else goes wrong."

She twisted to face him. "Since when do you know so much about plumbing?"

"Mike's dad's always botching a job." His frown spread to a crooked grin. "We just laugh."

"Stop laughing at people's attempts to save money, Bran. You need to think about that yourself. I'm not an ATM machine." She pushed one knee to the floor, grasp the sink rim and rose. "Why are you late? I've been home from work for an hour, and I'm at the school longer than you."

"I watched baseball practice." He looked away, his expression growing belligerent. "I'd be playing ball if you'd get off my back, Mom. The doctor's have more faith in me than you have. I've been great for two years. I got energy, and—"

"Then how about helping out around here." She swung her arm toward the backyard. "The flowers will never grow underneath all those autumn leaves that you were supposed to rake last October."

Brandon pivoted on his heel and marched through the doorway into the dining room. "Forget it. You'll never understand."

She listened to his footsteps thump down the hall followed by the slam of his bedroom door. Lately they'd been at odds, and no matter what she did, according to Brandon, was wrong. Her income working in the high school office didn't buy them steaks and designer jeans. She'd learned to budget and watch her pennies. Brandon expected her to be his financier and housekeeper. When Tom died, life changed. Not only had she lost her husband, but Brandon had lost his father. She understood girls. Boys, she didn't.

Ava sank onto a kitchen chair, eyed the wrench and set it on the table. Now that she started the plumbing job, she wished she hadn't. Brandon had been right. She'd resolved the faucet leak, but now water dripped under the sink. She felt stupid. If she'd taken Quinn's offer, everything would be fixed. But taking advantage of his kindness wasn't her way.

Pulling up her shoulders, she rose and headed down the hall to Brandon's room. She stood a moment before giving the door a tap. "Bran. Let's talk."

"Thanks anyway." His deep mumble penetrated the door.

Her little boy had vanished a year ago, maybe last summer between his fourteenth and fifteenth birthdays. He'd shot up three inches, and she had to look up at him now. He used to let her kiss his cheek and give him a hug. That ended with the growth spurt. All she got now was "Mommmm" spread out as if the letters were on grease. She missed the affection.

Her pulse tripped again as Quinn's face dangled in her

thoughts. She'd tried to push it aside. Life kept her too busy to deal with a man. A woman needed enough time and energy to develop a relationship with someone. She shook her head. What made her think the man had an interest in anything other than helping with her plumbing. Why had she stressed she tried to save money? She didn't want Quinn's pity.

"Brandon." She knocked harder. "Open the door."

It flew open, startling her. Brandon glanced at her, then pointed toward the window. "There's some guy looking at the house. I've been watching him."

"Some guy?" She followed him across the room to the front of the house, and when she looked out, her heart stopped. "Oh, my."

"What's that mean?"

"I know him." She dropped the edge of the curtain. "That's the man who backed into me."

"You mean the fender-denter?"

She wanted to wash the smug look from his face. "I meant bender and you know it." Why did she keep calling it that? And why was Quinn out there? Her pulse clipped to a trot.

"He's probably a nutcase." He strutted for the door. "I'll tell him to get his—"

"Brandon, no." Her heart knotted in her throat. "I'll take care of it."

He spun around. "Look, Mom. I'm the man in this family and—"

"And I'm your mother. Thank you, but I'll take care of it." She strode toward the door, then stopped. "And he's not a nutcase."

"Right."

She ignored his sarcasm and continued to the front door, but when she grasped the knob, she paused. Seeing him sitting in his car at the curb had sent her over the edge. With her lungs on overload, she gasped for air. *Focus. Focus.* Her mind raced to find a logical explanation as to why Quinn had parked in front of her house. It wasn't a coincidence. That she was certain.

Plying her courage, she pulled open the door and stepped onto the porch.

As soon as he noticed her, Quinn stepped from the SUV and headed up the sidewalk. "Sorry. I should have called."

"How do you know where I live?" She forced her voice past her constricted lungs.

A frown broke on his face. "Well, I…"

His discomfort caught her off guard.

"I looked… There aren't any other Ava Darnells in the white pages."

"You looked in the phone book?" Her pitch had raised a notch. "Why?"

He evaded her eyes for a moment, then gave her a direct look. "I wondered about your plumbing and about your car. I see you got it back. It looks great."

"It does. Thanks." Ava tugged on the hem of her blouse. "Quinn, I… That wasn't a very warm greeting. You surprised me." Her emotions had waged a war between temptation and concern. "I'm glad you stopped in. I repaired the leak, but now I have another problem." She grasped the knob. "Would you like to come in?"

He faltered. "Is it okay?"

She nodded and opened the storm door, beckoning him inside.

As she stepped in behind him, Brandon stood in the hallway door, scrutinizing their guest. "This is my son. Brandon, this is Mr. O'Neill."

Quinn extended his hand while Brandon eyed it a moment before accepting his handshake. "So, you're the guy who ran into my mother."

His accusatory tone seemed to throw Quinn. He did a double take, his gaze searching hers and then flying back to Brandon.

"Bran, apologize." She tilted her head toward Quinn. "It was an accident."

Belligerence darkened his face. "I'm sorry you hit my mother's car." He spun on his heel and headed into his room.

Ava's jaw sagged, and she stood gaping at the empty doorway before regaining her wits. "I apologize for my son. He's in a little snit today, and he's taken it out on you." She stepped toward the hallway. "I'll tell him to—"

"Please, don't." He peered past her. "Is the kitchen that way?" He gestured toward the dining room archway.

She nodded. "Follow me." Ava strode ahead of him, wanting to barge into Brandon's room and give him a piece of her mind, but Quinn had asked her to drop it. She'd handle Brandon later.

Quinn walked to the sink and eyed the faucet. "I don't see the problem."

His relieved expression confused her until she realized he hadn't heard what she'd said. "It's a new situation. I'm afraid I did something wrong when I repaired the faucet. Now I have a drip under the sink." She opened the door and motioned inside.

He stared at it a moment before crouching down and peering in.

She sensed Quinn didn't want to get dirty, because he only reached inside to feel the pipes. Finally he shoved his head beneath the sink farther, then knelt and reached back into the cabinet. "I think I spot your problem."

"Really?"

"Did you use the sprayer recently?"

She studied him, not understanding his question. "I often use it to rinse dishes or the sink."

"I'm sure it's the hose on your sprayer. That's where the water's dripping." He drew his head from beneath the cabinet, accomplishment filling his face. "Probably a small hole or crack in it. After you use it, you'll find the water."

Her heart melted. She'd never seen his full smile, his blue eyes twinkled and lines crinkled above his cheeks like George Clooney.

"Listen." He rose from his crouch, his smile fading. "I have to be honest."

Honest? She froze. What would he spring on her now?

"I don't know a thing about plumbing, but I do think it's the hose. They're flexible tubing—plastic, I think—and I suppose they wear out in time."

He didn't know a thing about plumbing? The admission threw her. "But you offered to come over and take a look."

He shrugged. "I wanted to help."

Embarrassment heightened his skin tone, and it made her smile. "Thanks for spotting the problem. That should be easy to fix."

"You think so?" He gave her a questioning look.

"I can fix it." Brandon's voice surged into the room before he appeared.

Quinn jerked his head toward him. "Great. It's nice your mom has a man to help around the house."

Brandon's eyes narrowed as he studied Quinn. "Yeah, I am the man of the house, but can you convince her of that?"

Once again, Brandon had stopped Quinn in his tracks. The boy needed a little fatherly discipline. He rubbed his hands together, then shoved one in his pocket. "I suspect your problem is solved." He took a step toward the kitchen door. "I should go."

Before Ava could stop him, Quinn gave a wave and strode toward the front of the house. She spun around to face Brandon, then swallowed her anger, but by the time she recovered her footing, Quinn had reached his vehicle and climbed in. She returned to the kitchen to speak with Brandon, but he had vanished, too.

She sank into the kitchen chair again, trying to sort out what had happened. Brandon could be mouthy with her, but she'd never seen him act that way with others. The incident roiled in her mind until the reason struck her. Brandon resented Quinn in the house. She'd never anticipated that kind of reaction from him. Never.

Chapter Three

Quinn studied the vinyl siding brochures and then examined the samples Ross had brought over for him to view. Though presently the wood trim had white paint, he liked the idea of a color, and vinyl meant no more painting. "I didn't know beige had so many shades."

Ross chuckled and leaned over to point to a lighter color. "This one is great with the dark brick you have here."

"It caught my eye when I first looked at the chart." He closed the brochure and leaned back. "Let's go with that." With Ava and her son still on his mind, Quinn's concentration wobbled as he talked about the house improvements. He'd thought Sean was demanding at times, but he'd never seen him rude to strangers. Brandon, on the other hand, had been rude.

Ross jotted notes on his clipboard and straightened his back. "All right, the trim is settled. What about the windows?"

Windows were the last thing on Quinn's mind.

Ross pulled some brochures from his case. "The first decision is the style of windows."

Choices? Quinn went blank.

Ross handed him the information. "Look them over. These

are tilt-in windows. No climbing ladders to clean them." He pointed to a section of the flyer.

Having just looked out his dirty windows, Quinn peered at the pamphlet while his concentration dueled with the multiple thoughts racing through his mind. He lowered the brochure, deciding to open up to Ross. "Yesterday, I dropped by Ava's to check on her plumbing."

Ross gave him a questioning look.

"It's a long story. Anyway while I was there, I noticed how attractive her house is. Too feminine for me, but it's Ava. Colorful yet cozy. Organized, yet homey. But I never had a chance to ask her about helping with my decor." He explained the plumbing issue and Brandon's rudeness. "I didn't know what to do so I left. I'm not a man who feels inept, but I did. I know she was embarrassed so I decided to leave and end the problem."

Ross shook his head. "I doubt if that ended the problem."

"What do you mean?"

"If Brandon is rude to you, then it's probably happening with his teachers, the principal." He shrugged. "And rudeness hurts his mother, too."

"But my hands were t—"

"The boy might be uneasy with another male in the house? You mentioned Brandon told you he was the man of the house."

Quinn caught his breath. "But the kid knows I'd only met his mother a few days before."

Ross looked out the window as if searching for a response in the landscape. Quinn followed his gaze. Two squirrels skittered up a tree and down again. A goldfinch landed on the bird feeder, his bright feathers adding color to the yet drab landscape. Though spring had arrived, it hadn't notified Royal Oak.

Ross refocused on Quinn. "Maybe he saw you as a threat."

A scowl pulled at Quinn's face. "You're kidding."

"His mother likes you. Brandon knows how to handle his mother, but he doesn't know how to handle you."

Quinn lost him at "his mother likes you." "She barely knows me."

Ross arched a brow. "I talked with her at the POSK meeting. I know she likes you. Maybe the boy was jealous. You'd be competition for her attention."

Needles prickled Quinn's spine. Competition? Jealous? And Ava liked him. "I don't want to cause trouble between her and Brandon, and I might if I ask her about helping me with the decorating. I'd thought she'd be a good choice."

Ross nodded. "She has the ability. I'm sure she's available." He glanced down at his hands. "And she can use the money."

"But she's proud."

He nodded. "Working for money is a whole different situation, isn't it?"

Quinn threaded his fingers together and rested them on the table. "I should call her then."

"I would. She can say no, but I think she'll say yes."

Relaxing his fingers, Quinn pulled his hands apart. "Okay, I will." The tightness in his shoulders lessened. "Now that I have that settled—" he grinned at Ross "—let's pick out some windows." He grasped the brochures again and opened the one on top.

The unbelievable filled Ava's mind as it had since yesterday when Quinn walked out in the wake of Brandon's insults. She planned to talk with him after Quinn left, but she thought better of it. She'd never seen Brandon in such a tiff, and she settled on the idea of letting him cool off. But she couldn't continue to ignore his behavior.

Today he'd asked to do homework at Mike's house after school, and though she sometimes questioned whether it was homework or monkey business, she tried to trust her son.

He'd been through so much. He'd missed weeks of school, lost his hair, gone through a year of treatments and sickness. Since he was twelve, he'd dealt with the fear of cancer, and finally he'd become a teenager who'd begun to think he had a future.

Still she was his mother, he needed guidance. Fifteen wasn't twenty-five. Two years in remission didn't guarantee a lifetime of good health. That fear laid her low. She needed faith in the doctors and the treatment. Lexie and Kelsey would say she needed faith in God.

She believed in Him, but her faith had drained with Tom's miserable scam investment, his sudden death and then Brandon's diagnosis. She'd talked with God so often with no response and asked Him questions He never answered. She'd begun to wonder if Jesus was only a prophet without almighty power as some claimed. But that was her "devil's advocate" at work. In her heart, she believed even though she hadn't been to church for years.

Maybe it was time to go. With her avoidance, she hadn't provided Brandon with a good role model of faith, either. She hadn't really thought of that until now. She'd done him a disservice.

Her stomach growled, and she wandered into the kitchen, not knowing if she should cook dinner for Brandon, too. Sometimes he was invited to eat at Mike's. As she opened the refrigerator, the telephone rang. Brandon. Relieved, she closed the door and grabbed the phone. Quinn's voice washed over her.

"I hope I'm not calling at a bad time."

Though her body belied her response, she assured him it wasn't.

"Good." His voice sounded more positive than it had the last time she'd seen him. "I wonder if you could do me a favor?"

Her mind whirled. "What kind of favor?"

"I'm having some refurbishing done on my home, and I recall your interest in decorating so I wanted to elicit your help...sort of your opinion."

Helping him was a change. Warmth spread through her. "Opinion about what?"

"I have no idea what colors work where." His voice rang with resignation.

"You want a woman's view on color schemes?" A grin stole to her mouth.

"That's it. The rooms are mainly beige."

Safe and muted like he seemed to be. She'd opened her life like a book, and he'd handed her a locked diary. "You'd like a little color in your life." She listened and heard nothing. "I mean color in your home."

"In my life is correct. I'm as drab as the house."

Her pulse skipped, hearing the tone of his voice. She had no inkling whether he was toying with her or being serious. "When do you want to talk?"

"Tomorrow? Could you take a look?"

Saturday. "That'll work." Her thoughts wavered as they settled on specifics, and when she hung up, she stood a moment grasping what she'd agreed to do. Quinn had asked for her opinion. He'd invited her to his home. He considered her ideas worthy. Instead of problems, the offer gave her something different to think about. She stretched her back, hoping to relieve the stress she'd felt earlier. It failed.

Wishing she could let her worries go, she eyed the clock again. Seven-fifteen. No Brandon. Though she wasn't the kind of mother who called his friends, today she headed for the phone. From the list tacked on the square of corkboard beside it, she punched in Mike's number and waited. The ringing stopped, and she heard a woman's voice.

"This is Ava Darnell, Brandon's mother. Could I speak with him a moment?"

"I'm sorry. Brandon's not here."

Her chest constricted. "Is Mike there? Maybe he knows—"

"No, Mike's gone, too. They went to Bill's."

Ava closed her eyes. She'd never heard of Bill. Her pulse raced as she hung up. Brandon had lied to her, and she'd never questioned him. Her trust crumbled. She eyed the kitchen clock. Seven-twenty. Ava sank into a kitchen chair and rested her chin in her hand. Who was Bill? And where did he live? Were they even there? Bill might have told his mother he was at Brandon's.

Defeat anchored her to the chair as disappointment turned to tears. Struggling to get a grip, she grabbed a napkin from the holder and brushed moisture from her eyes. Determined to take hold of the problem and resolve it, she forced herself from the chair and opened the refrigerator. Although eating ranked with having a molar pulled, she needed to do something, and it was past dinnertime.

A couple of chicken breasts sat thawing on the refrigerator shelf, and she pulled them out. As she cut the meat into strips for a stir-fry, her hand jerked at the sound of the door opening. She closed her eyes a moment, a prayer escaping, and her breathing hitched at the surprise. She hadn't prayed in years.

Sensing Brandon's presence, she peered over her shoulder.

He stood in the doorway, watching her. "What's for dinner?"

Her first response caught in her throat. She swallowed the "nothing for a liar." Instead she lowered the knife and faced him. "Stir-fry."

Brandon's nose wrinkled.

Her shoulders ached with tension. "Where have you been? I thought you were doing homework with Mike?"

His brows lifted. "I was."

"Mike wasn't home. His mother said he was at Bill's." Clenching her hands at her sides, she watched the blood drain from his face.

His eyes searched hers, and then the color returned, the shade of a lobster. "Don't tell me you called Mike's house."

She glared back at him. "You lied to me."

"No, I didn't. Me and Mike did our homework at Bill's and then we hung around." His eyes narrowed. "I can't believe you're treating me like a child. Mom, I'm fifteen. I'm not a baby. I'm tired of being treated like one."

"You're fifteen not twenty-one, Brandon. I'm responsible for you. I care about you, and I'm your mother. Don't forget it."

He lowered his eyes, his head swaying. "You won't let me forget it. You'll never let go. I'll be a child until I die…which might be sooner than you think."

Sooner? Her heart stopped. "What's wrong?" She stepped toward him, her tension overtaken by weakness. "Did you find a lump? Where is it?"

"Stop, Mom." His voice resounded against the walls.

Her legs trembled, as she tried to make sense of what had happened.

Brandon's hands flew to his face. "I can't believe this." He stood a moment, then inched his fingers from his closed eyes, his body rigid. "I haven't found any lumps, but I'd rather be dead than live a life of the constant reminder that I might have my cancer return. You won't let it go, Mom. You care about the disease more than you care about me."

She drew back, startled at his response. "No, Bran. No. You're the most important thing in my life."

"No, Mom, that can't be, because you don't have a life. You're living mine. Please, let me grow up. Let me be a teenager like the other kids." He caught his breath, the color draining again from his face. "You want to know what I was doing after the homework?" He tugged his backpack from his shoulder. "And I can show it to you. It was my geometry, and we studied for a history test."

Her head spun with the confrontation, a horrible new experience that she never wanted to face again. "Bran, I believe you. I'm sorry." But his look told her it was too late.

"I'll tell you what else we were doing." His jaws tightened. "We played basketball at Bill's. He has a hoop on the garage. You can ask his mother. I jumped and ran. I had fun, Mom, and I feel fine. Better than fine. I feel great."

Tears welled in her eyes, and she choked on the sob caught in her throat. Her head spun with remorse, but as much with love she didn't know how to express anymore. He wouldn't let her. She sank into the nearest chair and covered her eyes, unwanted tears rolling down her cheeks.

Brandon stood over her, his hand a fleeting touch on her shoulder before he plopped into the seat she'd vacated earlier. "I'm sorry, Mom. I guess you're trying to be a good mother, but…I don't know…I want a chance to live before I don't have a chance."

Her head bobbed up, the look on his face ripping at her heart. "Don't say that, please. You're going to be fine."

"I don't think you believe that." His whisper swept past her.

"Bran, I do believe it with my heart, but sometimes I worry. Things haven't gone well with us. Dad and then your diagnosis. Sometimes I think God has forgotten us."

"God?" A frown lay on his brow, his mouth curved down. "You're not religious. You never talk about—"

"That's another of my mistakes. I do believe, but as I just said, sometimes I think God's given up on me."

"He doesn't do that."

Her head jolted upward. "What?"

"Mike's family goes to church. They say prayers at meals, and I've heard them talk about their faith. They're so confident I guess it rubs off."

Her pulse raced. "I've done you an injustice, Bran. If we lean more on God and less on each other, maybe we can sort things out."

His dark expression vanished, and hope filled his eyes. He rose and took a step to her side. "Mom, I didn't mean to—"

"I didn't, either, but this was good. We've let too much come between us. Since we're really communicating, I want to mention your attitude toward Mr. O'Neill yesterday. I was embarrassed, and I'm sure he felt the same." Quinn's expression dangled in her mind as it had since the situation happened. He looked at a loss.

"I took my frustration out on him, and I'm sorry if I embarrassed you, but you don't really know that man, Mom. Did you ever think he could be a crook or something?"

"A crook? Why would you say that?"

"He could be using you." He waved his hand in the air. "You know, he bumps you, becomes a friend and then tries to rip you off."

"Rip me off of what?" Her pulse surged.

"Your money."

"What money?" Ava rose and stood face-to-face with Brandon. Her energy failed her, and she braced herself on trembling legs. "If a man is stalking a woman for money, he'd pick someone with a big house and fancy car." She gestured to the kitchen. "No stainless-steel appliances here. He'd be crazy to swindle a woman in a slab house with three small bedrooms."

"Okay, Mom. I made a mistake. If you run into each other again, tell him I'm sorry."

She shook her head, trying to clear it. "Are you trying to be funny?"

He shrugged. "I wanted to make you smile."

Brandon slipped his arm around her shoulders. It had been so long. Jubilant, she hugged him back. Still the problem remained, but he'd admitted he'd been wrong and that was a start. When she drew back, she looked into his eyes. "I know this won't end our disagreements, but I hope we can remember that talking it out is better than holding it in."

He nodded and stepped back, his gaze drifting from hers. "I'll try to think before I speak."

"I hope so, but thank you." She squeezed his shoulder before returning to the chicken. "Stir-fry might not be your favorite but—"

"It's fine, Mom. Everything's fine."

She tucked his words into her heart while another prayer lifted heavenward.

Quinn stared out the living-room window, anticipating the unfamiliar experience of having a woman in his home. And not any woman. Ava. She'd carved a deep trench in his mind, and periodically he fell into it. He struggled getting out. He'd analyzed the situation. First he thought about the accident that roused his sense of responsibility. Then he considered her son, and the impact the boy had on him—definitely a negative one—but it took him back to his fifteen-year-old son. When out of his earshot, Sean may have been rude, too.

Weighted by options, Quinn accepted the truth. Ava appealed to the man in him. He'd been without a woman in his life for four years, and though he'd faced his family's deaths, he hadn't faced the reality. He hadn't died with them, and now he wanted to live again. The house's renovation mirrored his need to make changes in his life, too.

A noise alerted him, and his pulse skipped when he saw Ava's car parked in his driveway. She remained in the car a moment as if getting her bearings before facing him. He supposed he deserved that. He hadn't been as genial as he should have been. Being more outgoing added one more way he had to change.

As she approached the door, he strode to the foyer, and when the bell rang, he hung back a moment. He didn't want her to think he'd been clinging to the doorknob waiting for her even though that's what he'd been doing. When he thought enough time had passed, Quinn pulled open the door.

His voice failed him when she offered him the brightest smile he'd seen from her. Her hazel eyes sparkled, and her cheeks blossomed with color as he pushed back the door.

She stepped inside, and though no words had been spoken between them, he understood. Interest filled her face as she shifted her eyes from the open staircase to the cathedral ceiling and the length of the foyer toward the family room. She looked side to side, taking in the living room and dining room from one spot. "Magnificent, but you're right. Beige paint must have been on sale."

He sputtered a laugh with her unexpected quip, and her surprised expression pleased him.

Her gaze swept the rooms. "This is a gorgeous home, Quinn. Really lovely and so charming. When was it built?"

He nodded, almost embarrassed when he thought of her much smaller house. "Nineteen twenty-one, when they made them sturdy."

"How long have you lived here?"

Her questions seemed unending. "Only three years."

"And you did the decorating?"

"No." He flinched. "It was like this when I moved in. I'd meant to—"

"Redecorate. Add a little of yourself." Her gaze caught his with a look that probed his thoughts.

His shoulders sagged. He didn't have a taste to add to the house. He'd ignored his last home, accepting his wife's choices. He'd ignored many things when he moved—to get away.

Quinn dug deep to lighten the conversation. "I'm slow when it comes to change. Think snail."

She chuckled, and the sound rang through the rooms and echoed up the staircase. Laughter. He drew it in, filling his memory with the joyful sound and relishing in a new energy. A grin clung to his mouth, and enjoying the wonderful release, he grasped for something else to add—lighthearted and free.

Instead her smile dimmed. "Thanks for the laugh. I needed that." Her admission caught him off guard.

Her gaze lowered to the floor as she drew up her shoulders. "But enough about that. Where do you want me to begin?"

His mind had been milling with dark thoughts. But her openness rallied him forward. "How about a tour of the house?" The image of her cozy house swept through his mind.

"I'd like that."

"I don't think I told you that I was impressed with your home. Very attractive. I saw you in the decor, and I also recognized your talent. You have a good eye for detail. An eye I don't have." Seeing the pride in her face sent a warm feeling rushing through his chest. He gathered his thoughts and gestured toward the rooms on each side of the foyer.

He surveyed her admiring expression as she stepped into each room—a slight lift of an eyebrow with a faint upward curve of her lips, a generous grin and approving nod. He felt reborn.

In the family room, her focus rose to the cathedral ceiling, and she spent time in the kitchen, eyeing the layout and commenting on the expansive counter space. His use of the kitchen was comparable to the whirlpool tub in the master bedroom. The shower served him just fine.

When they reached his study and his master suite next door, Ava studied him while she tapped her finger on her lips, today the color of ripening cherries. He closed his eyes to control a wave of sensations. Regret. Longing. Hope. He opened his mouth to ask her opinion but faltered. She would offer her opinion when ready—and he'd hear plenty. The reminder made him grin.

Though he used the second floor only for storage, a few

mementoes of the past, Ava wanted to view the rooms. At the top of the stairs, she took stock of the layout before perusing the four bedrooms and two baths. When she'd finished, she turned toward him and shook her head. "You could open a bed-and-breakfast with all this space."

"After one of my breakfasts, I'd be out of business. Maybe a shelter for the homeless. They would appreciate cold cereal and coffee or a frozen entrée for dinner. That's all I know about cooking."

She chuckled before she turned and descended the stairs.

At the bottom of Quinn's staircase, Ava's head spun. The place equaled some of the loveliest homes in the prestigious areas of Oakland County. Good-looking and available, he lived in this magnificent house alone. Why had he never married? The questions kept coming. Her fingers curled into a knot as if the tight fist could keep her curiosity under wraps. "Do you want to talk now?"

He arched a well-shaped brow. "Why not?" Quinn motioned toward the family room, so she turned down the hallway and stepped into the vast room with a homey fireplace and lovely windows that looked out into what had been a garden, a beauty, she guessed. Apparently Quinn didn't know much about landscaping, either. His plumbing issues plunged into her mind along with his admission of knowing nothing about cooking. So what did he know?

When she stepped through the foyer into the family room, he motioned toward a chair. He remained standing, and she looked at him a moment before sinking into the soft leather.

"Would you like something to drink? Coffee? A pop?" He'd strode toward the archway into the kitchen.

"I'm fine, but thanks."

He shrugged and vanished through the doorway while she looked past the fireplace to the view out the window. The garden could be lovely if cared for. She enjoyed planting flowers and always longed for a place to do real landscaping instead of putting a few annuals along the porch edge. Her gaze drifted over the saddle-brown leather sofa and the straight lines of the furniture. No photographs or artwork hung on the walls, nothing personal to give her a clue about his taste. She lowered her eyes when Quinn's muted footsteps hit the carpet.

He headed toward her, carrying two glasses of water and set one on the table beside her. "Just in case."

She gave a nod, pleased he'd considered the possibility she would change her mind. Though tempted to ignore the glass, she grasped it and took a sip. The refreshing liquid washed down her dry throat. "Thanks." She leaned back and scrutinized him. Adding color to someone's home meant knowing the person, and she didn't know one thing about Quinn other than what he couldn't do.

The silence brought a frown to his face.

"Quinn, what are your interests? What do you do for fun? I don't even know what you do for a living."

His frown deepened. "Why do you need to know that?"

"You said it yourself. A home reflects who you are." The smile lines she'd admired had faded.

"I want something different, that's all. Something brighter." He looked away, his gaze drifting to the garden window. "I need a landscaper, too. The garden is pitiful."

She'd rattled him, and he'd changed subjects. Ava wouldn't let him do that. "What do you do for a living? That can reflect a little about you."

His eyes snapped back to hers. "I'm in software."

"Software." Although surprised, she wasn't sure why. He could be anything for all she knew. But software meant he had technical skills, a mind that worked through complex problems. "Interesting." He'd probably be organized and detailed. "Where's the company? Close by?"

His gaze penetrated hers. "I'm not sure why that makes a difference, either."

"The closer you are to your place of employment the more leisure time you have. It means you have more time at home for your interests." His closed-mouthed manner irked her.

His face grew blank. "Grand Rapids."

"That's almost three hours from here, isn't it?"

"Yes, and before you ask, I'm able to work from home most of the time." His tone grew edgy.

"Understanding your way of life—your lifestyle—helps me sense who you are." She liked answers, but she certainly wouldn't ask why he didn't live in Grand Rapids. Trying to learn any more about him seemed hopeless. She felt as inept with him as she did with Brandon. Maybe it was a man thing.

Quinn waved his hand through the air. "Listen. I didn't mean to be short with you." He straightened against the chair cushion and shifted his legs. "I don't care if the house looks like me, whatever that might be. All I care about is it's clean and has a little color. Something to look at other than beige."

She reached for the water, then withdrew her hand. "This doesn't seem to be a good day for our talk. I'll pick up some color samp—"

"Ava, I'm sorry. I don't like talking about myself."

"I noticed." She rubbed her temples, her mind asking why. "I should be more patient and not push you, but I've felt as if I'm hanging over the edge of a cliff."

"Have I caused that?"

"A little." A sigh stole from her lungs. "Mainly, it's Brandon."

A tight frown coursed his face. "Is it the Hodgkin's?"

"No, not that." His question explained his look. "He told me he was going to his friend's house and that's not where he went." The admission made her wince.

Quinn tilted his head. "How did you find out?"

Guilt snaked through her as she gave him the short version, and when she finished, his look left her confused. She grasped her handbag and braced her feet to rise. "I'll pick up the—"

"Wait."

She froze with his command.

"Brandon's becoming a man. I know that's hard to believe, but he's seeking independence, and like most teens, when they feel held back, they—"

She sank into the cushion, her frustration rising. "But I'm his mother. I have a right to know where my son is and what he's doing."

"You do, but you've reined him in too tightly." He leaned forward. "Try giving him some freedom, and he'll stop tugging to get loose."

She tensed.

"You worry about his health and you're letting that control your parenting. Ask yourself about what's best for him. Loosen the leash, and show him you trust him."

Loosen the leash. What did he know? She braced herself, trying to control her irritation. "I realize I'm concerned, very concerned about his health, but who are you to tell me how to raise my son?"

Quinn flexed his hand upward. "Ava, please. I'm offering some ideas, that's all. I know how boys can be. They want to be men before they're ready, but they need to test it out a little or they'll never learn. It's hard to be a good parent and not—"

"Wait a minute." She tugged her bag to her shoulder and stood. "I realize you were a boy once yourself, but you're not a parent. I don't see any kids here. Those bedrooms are empty. Who lives in this big house?" Her arm made a wild arch past the empty rooms. "You live alone. What do you know about raising a son?"

His eyes pierced hers. "I had a son once."

His voice cut through her ire and knocked her back into

the seat. "You had a son?" Her mind splintered. "You're divorced?"

"I'm a widower."

She grappled with his admission.

"My son died in the same car accident as his mother." He rose, his face mottled with emotion. "And you're right. Let's forget this." He lifted his arm and swung it from side to side as if he were erasing the moment.

Ava's heart plunged. Pain and sorrow exploded on his face. She stared in shock, and though she wanted to apologize for her outburst, the daunted look in his eyes stopped her from saying anything. She wanted to leave, to run into the spring sunshine and melt her icy regret, but she couldn't when he needed to talk, to unlock the pages of his life. Heavyhearted, she envisioned the beautiful empty home and asked herself, What could she do now?

Chapter Four

Quinn gazed up at his office building, pride growing in his chest as he strode through the parking lot to the entrance. Thoughts of his talk with Ava had filled the two-and-a-half-hour ride to Grand Rapids. He'd owed her an explanation after his outburst, so he explained how the drunk driver had swerved into the lane and hit his wife and Sean head-on. He should have told her the whole story—get it out in the open— but he couldn't admit his argument with Sean and then Lydia insisting on taking him to practice driving. Each time the memory assailed him, he relived the torment of their deaths.

He would never have volunteered to tell her what had happened, but Ava had a way of dragging things out of people with her incessant questions. Sometimes he resented them, but he needed to let it go, and in a strange way, she'd done him a favor. The Lord said to lay life's burdens on Him, but he had an awful time doing it.

He and Ava had finally returned to the topic of decorating his house. He told her about a few of his interests and answered more questions. Though she'd seemed content, he'd sensed that the earlier frustration they'd felt had put a damper on the rest of her visit. Ava couldn't hide her emotions. They sparked in her eyes.

The spring day sent warmth through him, but when he stepped into the building, an unexpected chill ran through him. He'd given his time and energy to the business, and sometimes he faced the damage his dedication had caused. He'd distanced himself from his son and even Lydia at times. Every ounce of energy went into building the corporation into a dynamic software business that created unique programs for companies around the world. Yet as he crossed the lobby toward the elevator, he felt lonely until Ava's image overtook his thoughts.

His chest constricted. He'd thought of her as attractive, but moments happened when she'd revealed her unique beauty. Beyond good looks, she glowed—her desire to understand, her honesty, her strength even in the dark times. It added to the depth of who she was. The Bible said that man looked at the outward appearances, but God looked at the heart. He sensed the Lord had decided it was time for him to open his eyes, and when he did, he saw her as the Lord wanted.

The elevator opened, and Quinn stepped inside, seeing his reflection in the mirrored walls. Since he'd left Grand Rapids, his dark hair had added swatches of gray at the temples and creases had sprouted around his eyes. He had grown old without knowing it.

The elevator stopped, and the door parted. Quinn stepped into the hall, drawing in the scent and sight of the corporate offices—high-polished floors, brass accouterments, opaque glass windows in the office doors. With every step, he relived his time spent there. He paused outside his brother's office, acknowledging he should have made an appointment. But he didn't let that stop him. He grasped the knob, taking a moment to gather his thoughts before pushing open the door.

His brother, Liam, sat with his back to the door, his ear covered by the telephone receiver. When he heard the noise, Liam spun around, surprise on his face. He held up his index finger and then tilted his head toward a chair.

Quinn sank into the leather upholstery, listening to his brother settle a deal. He could see his likeness in Liam's face though a younger version. Liam's dark hair showed no hint of aging, and when he flashed Quinn a smile, his blue eyes sent him a wink. Only half listening to the familiar dialogue he'd engaged in for so many years, his attention shifted to the large window where the Grand Rapids skyline stood against a blue sky dotted with cirrus clouds. So unencumbered and serene. Quinn longed to feel that way.

The clink of the receiver drew him back. Quinn stood and grasped his brother's hand. "Busy, I see."

"So what do I owe this honor?" He rose and gave Quinn a one-armed hug. "You haven't been around for a long time."

"I know. If you need me, I'm only a phone call away." But he knew his brother better than that. He wouldn't admit being unable to handle the job. That's another way they were alike. "Do you have a minute?"

Liam motioned to the seat Quinn had vacated. "Sure."

As he sank back into his desk chair, Quinn withdrew to the visitor's chair.

"Everything okay?" The look on Liam's face spoke volumes.

"Doing well." That was a stretch, but better than he had been. "Business seems as if it's ticking like clockwork."

A smile grew on his brother's face. "I just closed a big deal with an international company. They have branches in Switzerland, Germany and Britain."

"I knew you could do this." Quinn had walked away from the day-to-day grind with confidence, and the longer he stayed away, the more he knew he'd done the right thing.

Liam's welcoming expression was replaced by a questioning look. "And that's why you came to see me?"

Quinn hadn't sorted out exactly why he'd come. "I suppose I wanted to see family."

"I know you, Quinn." He gave him a pointed look. "What's the problem?"

"Nothing. Things are looking up. Believe it or not, I'm getting some work done on the house."

Liam's eyebrows arched. "You're doing the work?"

"A contractor, and I—I've hired a woman to do some decorating." When he saw his brother's expression, he wanted to kick himself for mentioning Ava.

"A woman." Liam's eyes pierced his. "And you hired her?"

Heat rolled up Quinn's chest. "She's talented, and the contractor knows her."

His brother chuckled. "Finally."

Quinn acted as if he didn't understand, but Liam's expression spoke loud and clear. "Right. I'm finally doing some things to the house."

"You know that's not what I mean." Liam rose from the chair, rounded the desk, and slipped onto the mahogany surface. "I'm glad you've returned to the living, Quinn. It's been too long, and you know Lydia would want you to be happy." He rubbed his hands together. "How did you two meet?"

"You're making more out of it than there is." Quinn struggled to keep his emotions in check. "We only met a short time ago, but I will admit the meeting was eventful." Relaying the fender-bender story, he monitored his voice, hoping his brother didn't detect more than he was willing to admit. "She has a fifteen-year-old son."

Liam grimaced. "Difficult?"

Quinn doled out the details, the bad attitude, the boy's Hodgkin's battle and Ava's frustration. "He resented my helping her with the plumbing. That's one way she saves money."

His brother chuckled. "You helped? Hmm? Let me guess. You really are interested in this woman." Liam braced his hands on his knees and leaned closer. "It's obvious."

"No, I—" He stopped the lie. "I suppose there's no point

in denying it." Hearing his admission aloud made it too real. "But it can't work."

"Why?"

His brother's blunt question gave him pause. He didn't know why, and that was one of his motivations for talking with his brother. "I sense it."

"Does she know about Lydia and Sean?"

He nodded, not admitting he'd left out part of the details.

"You said you paid for her car repair. She knows you're wealthy, then."

The question dug deep. "I don't know. I didn't tell her I owned the business. She's never said anything and neither have I."

"Be careful, Quinn. Sometimes money is what motivates a relationship."

The comment hit him like a slap. "Why are you suspicious? I ran this business much longer than you have, and I think I know how to read people."

Liam shook his head. "Not when the heart is involved. I'm not trying to stir up problems, but be aware that those things happen. Love can blind a person."

"Who said anything about love?" His lungs emptied of air, but he managed to draw a breath. "Ava's independent. She said no about the car repairs more than once before I convinced her to let me pay. She worried about her premium going up, and now Brandon's eager to get his learner's permit which means added cost to her insurance to cover a teen driver."

Liam flinched with the reference. "Stay out of that situation. You don't need to get involved. It's too close to home. I know it's been four years, but you've only begun to heal. I worry about you, brother."

"You're my kid brother. I'm supposed to worry about you." But Liam's caution was a good one. "I'll beware. I know my limits when it comes to that, but I think your worries about

Ava are wrong." He studied his brother's expression. "But I'll keep it in mind. How's that?" But only for a minute.

"That's all I ask." Liam slipped from the desk and rested his hand on Quinn's arm. "One of these days I'll surprise you. Maybe Jen and I will take a ride over and look at the house."

"That would be great. I'd like that."

But he knew it wasn't the house that would draw his brother to Royal Oak. Ava was the calling card that motivated him. Though he resented his brother's advice, his concern let him know someone cared about him even if it was only his brother.

Ava slipped the receiver onto the front office phone and jotted an absentee note for one of the students who had a doctor's appointment the next day. She liked when parents called ahead. The student could pick up their return-to-class form in the morning without a hassle.

Arching her back, she faced her growing lack of patience. When she left Quinn's on Saturday, irritation had been her primary emotion but when his outburst settled into her mind, her heart surged with grief for a man who'd lost the two people he loved in one fleeting moment. Quinn's protection of his private life now cushioned her attitude. She understood.

The thought tempered her frustration with Brandon. Quinn had lost a son—a son who had turned fifteen as Bran had done—but she still had her boy. Even his serious illness seemed less horrifying than the death Quinn had faced. With Bran's remission, Ava's confidence and hope had lifted higher than it had since he was diagnosed, despite her negative tendency.

And today she'd understood what Quinn had been trying to say. She'd hung on too tightly to Brandon. While he wanted to regain the freedom he'd lost with his illness, she continued to remind him daily that he was still sick. The restrictions she demanded had discouraged his healing rather than allowing him to enjoy his health. She froze with the thought. But it was difficult to change. She could only try.

For so long, she'd placed her weak faith into a closet as she'd done with Tom's clothes after he died. She knew they were there, but she didn't look at them or touch them, but somehow it gave her comfort knowing part of him remained close. Disjointed thoughts and senseless worries had ruled her life. After Brandon's diagnosis, she'd cleared out the closet, but her faith remained in a dark corner.

The time had come to bring her faith out of hiding. She needed strength to give Brandon the leash, to trust and support him.

Quinn, too. He needed support, but she had no idea where he received it. He'd let his home become run-down. He attended church but didn't socialize. What kind of life was that? Though her own social life was limited, she attended the POSK meetings and had developed a few friendships with people like Lexie and Kelsey who knew her plight.

"Ava."

Her head bolted upward, and she looked into the eyes of her coworker Denise. "Sorry. Did you say something?"

Denise jerked her head sideways, and Ava saw Brandon standing at the office counter. She rose as tension settled in her neck. "What's up?"

He lowered his eyes. "I wanted to know if…" He lifted his head. "I don't suppose you'll let me, but Mike and I have a chemistry exam tomorrow and he asked me to spend the night so we could study together, toss questions to each other. If you don't trust me, you can—"

"I trust you, Bran." A weight constricted her chest as his questioning eyes widened leaving her filled with remorse. "Do you need a ride?"

His jaw loosened as he studied her. "No. Mike's mom will pick us up, and she said we could swing by the house so I can get what I need for tomorrow."

"Okay." She dug her approval from a deep place. "Could you call me before you go to bed?"

"Sure." A faint grin took the stress from his jaw. "Mothers worry."

"They do." She managed to smile back.

"Thanks, Mom. I'll call later." He spun around and headed through the office door, a bounce in his steps that she hadn't seen in a long time.

She settled back at her desk, delving into the attendance reports for the day and stacking the forms into a neat pile. But her thoughts didn't stay on forms or reports. She owed Quinn an apology, and despite the tense meeting she'd had with him on Saturday, he'd let her know he still wanted her decorating ideas. With Brandon busy, shopping beckoned her. The new plan lightened her spirit.

When the hour slipped to four o'clock, she turned off her computer, dug her handbag from her desk drawer and locked it before saying goodbye to Denise. Outside the late-April breeze reminded her that spring had finally arrived. Sunlight, new growth and freshly mowed grass wrapped around her senses. The warmth spread to her thoughts. Brandon was safe at his friend's home, giving her time to visit the home-supply store to look at paint colors and gather some decorating ideas.

She drove to Lowe's in Madison Heights and veered into the parking lot. Inside she located the paint display and delved into the colorful paint samples, comparing and contrasting while she thought about Quinn's interests. Nature was the one that came to mind. With a stack of samples in her hand, she strode toward the exit while pulling her cell phone from her bag. She dialed Quinn's number and waited.

Quinn hung the receiver on the hook and stepped back, his eyes shifting from one corner of his kitchen to another. Ava's call, though a welcome break in his silence, reminded him that he'd agreed to brighten his home and in the process brighten his life. The reality of the change set his teeth on edge. He wanted to be different, but could he? He'd jumped from workaholic to a near recluse following his family's deaths, and breathing life back into him sounded unreal.

Ava's enthusiasm sent his pulse racing. She blathered on about nature, paint colors, brightness and contrast. It meant nothing to him, but he'd agreed to have her drop by with paint chips. If he changed his mind, she would be disappointed. And so would he. Each change he made was a step closer to living a normal life again.

Suspecting Ava would be there soon, he put on a pot of coffee and wished he had a snack to offer her. He opened the refrigerator. A carton of milk, a few eggs and a loaf of bread. He pulled open the fruit drawer and found an apple that had withered to a shrunken head. Restaurants and frozen dinners kept him alive. In the cabinet, he located crackers and a can of tuna. Not much for a snack. He closed the cabinet and headed into the living room.

Aware of the warm day, Quinn opened the front door, allowing the spring air to filter through the foyer into the living room. The scent mingled with earth and newly mowed grass. His lawn spiked up in neglect. Another job he...or a landscaper...needed to handle.

As he stepped away from the doorway, Ava's sedan rolled into the driveway. His stomach tightened. His mind had become a jumble of longings, regrets and anxiety. Could peace find him again? Could love put color back into his world?

Ava waved as she headed up the sidewalk, wearing a welcoming smile as if the tension between them hadn't happened. He wished that had been true. As he pushed open the screen door, a sweet, soft sensation rolled through him. "Nice day, isn't it?"

"It is, and it's about time." She stepped through the doorway into the foyer, clutching her bag, the only sign of tension she'd failed to hide.

He nodded and motioned toward the living room. "Here or the family room?"

"Family room, I think."

Quinn waited for her to lead the way. The term "family room" made his heart ache. He hadn't been a family for four years. Even before he'd been only an insignificant part of his family's workings.

Ava settled on the sofa and set her bag beside her. "I'm anxious for you to see the paint samples." She pressed her lips together. "I know my tastes so decorating my own house was easy. This is a challenge."

"I'm looking for something different." Quinn grasped the back of his recliner. "That's about it. It'll be clean and—"

"But it should be more than clean. I want it to be attractive and reflect who you are." She searched his eyes. "I realize you don't care about that, but it's my pride, I suppose. I want to do a good job so when people visit and say that the decor is lovely, you can say Ava Darnell designed the room for you."

Ava had knocked his legs out from under him. "Ava, here's the problem." He swallowed as he forced the words to his throat. "I don't think I know who I am."

She drew back, her head tilting as if she wanted to soak in what he'd said but had no idea how to do it.

Quinn sank into the chair. "You know who you are. You're confident in what's important to you and where your life is headed." He pressed his palm against his chest. "I have no idea."

Her back sank against the cushion as she studied him. Silence permeated the room, so rare when Ava was present. If she weren't so serious, he could have chuckled. He remained quiet, too, wishing he could add more, and wanting to tell her that he longed to know where his life was going, but he couldn't.

She inched her back from the leather upholstery and captured his gaze. "Then it's time for you to figure it out." She released a sigh. "I don't want to argue again, Quinn. For some crazy reason, I like you. Don't ask me why."

Her admission toppled his growing argument.

"But I'm going to be blunt." Ava leaned even closer. "I haven't dealt with the death of a spouse and son as you did, but I lost a husband and have lived with a son who could die from cancer. That's what Hodgkin's lymphoma is, you know."

He gave a nod, unable to do more.

"I've grieved for years, but I managed to rein it in, to control the pain and sorrow by looking to the future. When we live in the past, we're stagnant. We can't grow or change because our feet are mired in things we can't control or change. All we can alter and make better is today."

He evaded her truth-filled eyes. He'd sunk into quicksand with nothing to hang on to when his faith died with his family that day. Yet he praised the Lord. He'd found his way back and God forgave him for his failure to trust. Yet he hadn't let go. He clung to his faith and the past as if it were a treasure.

With effort, Quinn lifted his eyes to Ava's. "You're right, but it's not easy, especially for a man who prides himself on being self-sufficient and able to deal with every serious issue he's had to face."

"All except one."

Her soft voice wove through his heart. "All except one."

"But you're ready to move ahead. That's what you told me the other day, and that's why I didn't let our unpleasant words stop me from following through."

Her spirit and honesty captured him. "And I thank you."

"Good." She gave him confident single nod. "Ready to talk paint?"

He hesitated and glanced at his watch. "It's nearly six. Is Brandon waiting for dinner?"

She lifted her shoulders and grinned as she related how she'd allowed Brandon to spend the night with Mike. "So thank you for your advice. I didn't like hearing it that day, but it was the truth. People don't always want to hear the truth."

"We don't, but I must admit you made some good points today yourself."

She looked away and nodded. "Thanks."

He rose and approached her. "Since Brandon's taken care of for the evening, let's head to downtown Royal Oak for dinner? We can talk paint later."

A smile answered his question.

Chapter Five

Ava sat beside Quinn, her mind filled with questions that she didn't want to ask him since it could ruin the evening. Quinn seemed to hate her questions, yet he'd opened up so much today. Why? Guilt? Regret for his previous nasty attitude? She released a sigh. What difference did it make? Opening up was what she'd wanted.

On the short ride down Main Street, she watched numerous well-known cafés and restaurants pass the window until finally Quinn pulled into a public parking lot. He stepped out, rounded the SUV and opened her door. Years had passed since anyone had been that gallant.

She smiled at him and stepped out of the vehicle, noticing her flat shoes and simple skirt and blouse. The local restaurants were both elegant and casual, and she hoped he'd chosen the latter, but when they strode back to Main Street, he paused at the door of Andiamo. Her spirit sank as she anchored her feet to the pavement. "Quinn, I'm not dressed appropriately for this place."

He drew back and made a full scan of her attire. "You look lovely. Why would you say that?"

She shrugged. "That's how I feel."

He gestured to his casual slacks and knit shirt before pulling open the door for her to enter.

Though she had qualms, she could do nothing now and stepped inside. Diners were scattered throughout the dining room with some tables along the windows and others more discrete. No one looked overdressed, and she calmed. Quinn had been correct. But the next item to arch her brows was the menu. The prices were far beyond what she could pay for even a special birthday or anniversary meal. And the salad cost extra. She stopped herself from gaping.

"See anything you like?"

Quinn's voice broke into her musing. She'd seen plenty that tempted her taste buds but paying that kind of money for dinner wasn't something she could do. "I'm still deciding. Everything looks wonderful." Relieved when her gaze lowered to the bottom of the menu, she relaxed. Simple pastas, some without meat, appeared with lower prices and included a salad. She found one she could handle. "I'll have the spaghetti in marinara sauce."

"That's it?" He lowered his menu. "I'm sorry I didn't ask you if you liked Italian food. That was my mis—"

"I love it. Really. I thought I'd eat a little lighter today." Her excuse sounded feeble.

"Instead how about the veal Parmesan? It's delicious." He pointed to it on her menu. "Ignore the fancy name they gave it."

She could ignore the fancy name but not the fancy price.

"This is my treat, by the way, and I'm having the filet." He tilted his head and studied her. "Do you like veal?"

She nodded.

"Then that's decided."

The waiter arrived and Quinn gave the order while she basked in the setting and Quinn's good looks. Curious, she tried to imagine having enough money to spend on a seventy-dollar dinner for two. She opened her mouth, then stopped.

How could she ask if he was rich? The only sign was this meal and his insistence on covering her car repairs which she'd tallied up to Christian kindness.

Instead of treading on dangerous ground, she pulled the paint chips from her handbag and set them on the table. "Take a look and see if any of these strike you."

He gazed at the cards for a moment before lifting them and shuffling through. "They're bright."

"Bright's popular now, but they're also tasteful. I selected tones that would complement each other." She pulled two cards from the stack. "For example, picture the adobe shade on one wall in the kitchen—probably the wall where the table sits in the bay window—and then cover the rest of the kitchen walls with the pastel caramel color. It's rich and warm and would look wonderful with the wood in your cabinets."

He grinned. "I'm not great at picturing things I can't see."

She shook her head, trying to imagine life without visual images. She saw Quinn in her mind daily. "I had two ideas for the bedroom. I stuck with nature. This topiary-green contrasting with the pale mint. It's restful and ties in with nature."

He nodded. "I trust you."

"You might be sorry you said that." His grin tickled her, but before she could respond, the salads arrived along with a huge pepper mill the waiter used to flavor the salads. She placed the napkin on her lap and picked up her fork, then noticed Quinn with his head bowed.

The prayer gave her a start although it shouldn't have. Blessing the food was natural for Christians. Recalling her recent thoughts to renew her faith, she lowered her head and sent a thank-you to the Lord for the food and also for meeting Quinn. If nothing more, he'd brought a new experience into her life and new stimulus. He picked her brain and respected her ideas. Even her husband hadn't done that for her. He'd taken her for granted as did Brandon now.

When she lifted her head, Quinn sat watching her. He grinned and joined her digging into the lush salad. A comfortable silence settled between them until his cell phone jarred the quiet. A frown rose on his face, and he pulled the phone from his pocket and eyed the caller ID. He sat still for a moment, then tucked it into his breast pocket.

Feeling uneasy, she motioned to his pocket. "If it's important, please answer the call. It won't offend me. I know you work from home. It could be your boss."

He looked away and chuckled before facing her. "I'm the boss, Ava. I own the company."

She swallowed her gasp. "I had no idea." Her mind spun again. Why did he live in Royal Oak when his business was in Grand Rapids? It didn't make sense.

Before she could untangle her thoughts, the phone rang again.

This time Quinn sat motionless.

"Quinn, please. It could be important."

He studied her a moment before pulling the phone from his pocket. He hit the button and slipped from his chair. "Stephen, I'm at dinner." He turned his back to her and walked away as he lowered his voice.

She concentrated on her salad, but her mind bogged with the phone call. Why did he leave the table? She realized it wasn't her business, but it reminded her of Tom and his clandestine phone calls that he covered with excuses. She'd been so naive then, believing her husband was telling the truth. Now she was too questioning sometimes even with situations that didn't involve her.

She looked Quinn's way, studying his face as he stood a distance from the diners. He tilted his head and nodded even though the caller couldn't see him. Before she looked away, Quinn eyed her a moment, a frown wrinkling his brow. Something caught in her throat, and she coughed. His glance caused her to feel like a voyeur even though she couldn't hear his conversation.

Finally Quinn slipped the phone back into his pocket and headed back to the table. When he settled into the chair, he looked stressed.

"Problems?" Too late to button her mouth.

Though he looked distracted, he shook his head. "No. Just some business matters. Nothing a little money shifting won't resolve." His face brightened as he dug back into his salad.

Ava's mind clicked with curiosity. Maybe his business was in trouble. Money shifting triggered old memories, and she pushed them from her mind. Yet Brandon's speculation returned with a jolt. He'd warned her that someone could look innocent and be a swindler, but not Quinn. She couldn't even imagine.

But that was why scams worked, wasn't it?

The door slammed, and Ava turned toward the kitchen doorway.

Brandon trudged in, his backpack slung over his shoulder. "I'm thirsty." He dropped his bag on the floor, opened the cabinet and drew out a glass.

Ava watched as he filled the tumbler with water.

He gulped it down, wiped his mouth with the back of his hand and set the glass in the sink.

"Hello." Ava arched a brow.

He shook his head. "Hi, Mom. I'm home." A snicker escaped him as he hoisted his backpack.

"Did you have a nice time?"

He shrugged. "I suppose."

"What did you do?"

A frown grew on his face. "We spent most of the time studying for our test."

With tension growing, Quinn came to mind. She hated

one-word responses and that's all she was getting from Brandon. "How did you do on the test?"

He shrugged again. "Okay, I think."

"That's it?"

"Mom, I won't know until tomorrow." He took a step toward the doorway.

"What did you do during the part that wasn't most of the time?"

Brandon pivoted, giving her a definite scowl. "Huh?"

"You said you spent most of the time studying. What else did you do?"

He lowered his eyes. "I knew it. Now I'm getting grilled. Are you a cop?"

She bit the edge of her lip. "No. Just your mother. I'm interested."

His shoulders slumped. "I shot some hoops." The look he gave her said, "There, now are you happy?"

Struggling to loosen the reins, Ava managed to smile. "Sounds like fun."

Brandon's expression froze. "It was." He stood a moment as if thinking it over, then headed through the doorway.

Ava crumpled into the nearest chair, giving herself a feeble pat on the back. Not perfect, but she'd tried. The problem was Bran looked tired and that frightened her. She buttoned her mouth, wanting to get through the evening without ruining the new "Mom" she wanted to be. It wasn't easy.

She opened the refrigerator and pulled out the pork chops. After trimming off the fat, she tossed them in a frypan, and while they browned, she peeled potatoes. Bran loved the meal she'd planned, and she hoped this would be another positive. Anything seemed better than what they had been going through.

With the potatoes in the water to boil, she opened a can of cream of mushroom soup and poured it over the chops. She added a splash of water in the pan, stirred to blend and covered the pan with a lid. A salad would finish dinner.

While she waited, she thumbed through the new home decorating magazine she'd picked up at the grocery store. Fresh ideas helped the creative process. She already knew she wanted to add some nature photos, and she hoped Quinn would let her find a few family photos to add to the decor. He would never forget his family so keeping them out of sight made the past more daunting. Quinn needed to find joy in the life he'd spent with his wife and son. Once accepting that part of his life, he could move on.

The scent of pork chops beckoned her, and she rose and gave it a stir, putting a fork against the tender meat. Perfect. She tossed a salad and mashed the potatoes, then headed down the hall. She tapped on Brandon's door. "It's time to eat."

Pressing her ear to the wood, she listened for a sound. "Dinner." Her pulse skipped as she gave another rap. "Bran, can I come in?"

Still nothing.

Holding her breath, Ava opened the door an inch and peeked inside. Bran lay on the bed, his face buried in his pillow. "Bran."

Her heartbeat quickened as she moved closer. "Bran?" She touched his arm.

Bran shot up like a rocket. "What?" Panic filled his eyes. "What's wrong?"

"That's what I want to know." She studied his face, fear growing. "Are you ill? Have you checked—"

"Mom." Brandon tossed his legs over the edge of the bed, his irritation evident. "I'm tired, that's all. We studied hard, and—"

"Did you stay up late?" Her fear and frustration came out of hiding. Angry that she'd succumbed to the old feelings again, she sank on the edge of his bed beside him. "I can't change overnight, Bran. I'm sorry. I…I'm trying."

His irritation melted and he slipped his arm around her back. "Forgiven." His head drooped downward for a moment, then he gave her shoulder a pat. "Thanks for letting me stay with Mike. I knew it was hard for you. And I'm fine. We stayed up until midnight. Mike's mom thought we were sleeping."

Memories flooded her with the days she was a girl and enjoyed sleepovers with friends. They'd yakked long into the night. She leaned her head against his muscular shoulder, realizing he was becoming a man. "I love you, Bran."

"Love you, too, Mom."

For a fleeting moment, she drank in the sweetness before rising and heading back into the kitchen.

Quinn eyed the newest financial report from his lawyer and slipped it into a drawer before checking his watch. Time had flown, and Ava would arrive in minutes, punctual as always. She'd called, and after they talked about the paint, she mentioned other decorating ideas she wanted to discuss. Now he wanted to pose the question of his garden. Ava said she enjoyed landscaping, and his needed a rebirth as much as he did.

His expectations of Ava took the wind out of him.

The doorbell rang.

Getting a grip on his emotions, Quinn straightened his frame, gathered his wits and headed for the door. When he pulled it open, he stood there, transfixed.

Ava looked like spring, short pants—he couldn't remember what they were called—a pale orange color that reminded him of a peach and a V-neck top with the same orange with white stripes. The color highlighted her rosy glow, and her brown hair glinted in the sunlight. She was trim but rounded, with flesh on her bones. He liked a woman of substance, both body and spirit.

"Can I come in?"

"Please." Stupefied, he stepped back.

Her smile spiraled to his core.

She stood a moment, her gaze drifting to the living room and then back to him. "I want to thank you again for the lovely dinner last week. My idea of going out is usually fast food."

He chuckled, but wondered if she meant it. Money always seemed an issue. His good life sat on his conscience like a wart on his nose. His mind shot to Judas, as it often did when thinking about the insurance money and the lawsuit. The chief priests used the thirty pieces of silver for a potter's field. Quinn worked hard to create his own kind of potter's field, but it never salved his guilt.

Ava strode into the living room, dropped her handbag on the coffee table and opened it. "What do you think?" She drew out a forest-green paint chip. "I think we should paint the whole room this color and use pure white for the wide chair molding and Adam's fireplace. It will be striking."

Quinn struggled to envision the dark green color covering all of the walls, but he recalled Ava's use of color at home, and it gave him confidence. "Interesting."

She studied his face, then proceeded to his sofa. "Look at this print. The same green is in the design. It reminds me of leaves in a forest."

Surprised that she'd noticed the color among the other shades of green, he gave her a thumbs-up. "Why don't you just surprise me with the rest?"

"You're kidding?" She drew back.

"No. I'm serious. Do you know a painter? I don't expect you to paint the walls yourself."

She rested her palm on his arm. "I do. Should I make the call?"

He managed to say yes though his mind had latched onto the touch of her hand against his skin. His memory surged back to the loving ministrations of Lydia, rubbing his back or giving him a gentle kiss. Until now, he hadn't realized how much he missed the touch of another human. The longing to embrace Ava overwhelmed him, but he only covered her small hand with his and gave it a pat.

Quinn needed a distraction. "How are you doing with Brandon?"

She blinked and sank onto the sofa. "Funny you should mention that."

Her expression aroused his curiosity. "A problem?"

"A problem resolved, thank goodness."

"You mean thank the Lord."

Surprise lit her face. "Sorry. That's what I meant."

He was sorry he'd made the comment. "I know you do." Yet Ava's distance from her faith bothered him. Though he admired Ava's strength, one day it could fail her, and she would have nowhere to turn without the Lord. "I'm glad you resolved it." He ambled to an easy chair and sat, anticipating she wanted to talk.

"I told you about letting Bran spend the night with a friend, but when he came home Thursday, he scared me and I bungled it."

Ava relayed the details of her encounter with Brandon. He sensed she wanted his advice, but words of wisdom failed him. He understood her concern and Brandon's resentment, but Quinn was at a loss when it came to worry. He'd let Lydia worry about everything at home while he focused on his company. She dealt with Sean's childhood illnesses, his cuts and scrapes, and his nightmares.

Realizing he'd failed his wife and his son had left him with a lesson. He wouldn't fail Ava. "It's natural to worry about him, and you did the right thing. It's great you settled it with a hug." A hug. Again his arms ached to hold her.

The distraction had been short-lived, and Quinn needed air and distance. He rose and pointed toward the back of the house. "You said you love to garden. Now that we've resolved the paint job, I'd like you to look outside and—"

"The painting isn't all we need to discuss, Quinn." A teasing gaze twinkled in her eyes as she rose. "You said decor not paint. Adding color to the walls is only part of it. Your walls are blank. Not one piece of art. Not one item on the table except a lamp." She shook her head. "Not even a plant, and you said you love nature."

"But…" He could see from her expression anything he would say would be useless. When he'd invited Ava into his life, he knew life would be different. Today, purpose washed away his emptiness. "Then you don't want to look at the mess outside?"

She chuckled. "I didn't say that, but I want to prepare you. You and I will do some shopping one of these days."

"Shopping? But—" He waved his hand to erase the word. Buts didn't work on Ava. "Fine. We'll go shopping."

Chapter Six

Ava hurried through the doorway of the POSK meeting room. Caught up in her worry about Brandon and the excitement of working on Quinn's renovations, she'd let time pass without noticing.

Kelsey beckoned her, and Ava settled beside Ross, the only empty seat near them. She refocused on Shirley Jackmeyer, the moderator, as she continued the meeting.

"One of our members wants to share a piece of news with you." Shirley waved to one of their newer members, and she rose and faced the group.

"We're all together in our struggle with our children's health issues, but I know you'll be thrilled to hear that my daughter Jackie has been given a clean bill of health."

Thunderous applause resounded through the room.

"And to celebrate, we've been given an amazing trip from Dreams Come True. My daughter's dream is to be a fashion designer, and we'll be spending a whole week in France attending the Paris ready-to-wear fashion showing. Jackie will have the opportunity to meet and talk with fashion designer, Elie Saab."

More applause followed her announcement, and Ava stifled her grin. She assumed Elie Saab was someone important, but her life was too far from designer clothes.

The meeting moved forward while her thoughts returned to Brandon. Though she longed to share her concern, she hesitated. So many others had situations far more dire than her niggling worries. She'd accepted Brandon's tiredness after spending the night at Mike's, but it happened two more times since Thursday. A red light flashed in her head. Fatigue was a symptom of Hodgkin's.

When Shirley's focus aimed at her, Ava was compelled to speak. "This is trivial compared to so many of your struggles, but—"

"Nothing is trivial, Ava." Shirley waved away her words. "When it weighs on our minds, we need to hand it over to our friends…and our Lord."

Ava shrunk with her message. How many times had she reminded herself to lay her burdens at Jesus's feet? "Thanks, Shirley. You all know that Brandon has been in remission for two years."

Applause and the buzz of comments scattered through the room.

She thanked them and then related her worry about Brandon's health and her struggle to monitor the trust factor between them.

Comments split the air—wait for more serious signs, call his doctor and ask his opinion, talk with Brandon and explain her concern. The advice that eased her fear came from Ross.

"Ava, trust Brandon. He knows his body and no one wants good health more than he does." Ross pressed his hand on hers.

She nodded, unable to speak through the lump in her throat. When she managed to swallow, she thanked those who offered their thoughts and wrapped her mind around Ross's words. Brandon knew his body. He wanted to be healthy.

Trust him. The thoughts turned into a prayer, and she laid it at Jesus's feet.

When the meeting ended, she stood, stretching the tension from her limbs. She'd been good at hearing others' needs, but she'd often kept hers inside. Letting them go today felt wonderful. "Thanks, Ross. That's the best advice you could have given me."

"You're welcome." He gave her a quick hug. "How's the work going with Quinn?"

Hearing his name startled her a little.

Ross frowned. "Not good?"

Ava found her voice. "No, it's fine. I hired a painter, and he's taking care of that task while I work on the landscaping."

Kelsey chuckled. "You're a Jill-of-all-trades."

"I'll have to prove myself for that title. He's given me full rein." The word stirred her thoughts to Bran's situation. "We're going to the nursery this Saturday."

Ross arched a brow. "I thought he gave you full rein."

"I insisted he help make decisions. I don't want all the responsibility if later he hates what I did." The conversation rolled through her mind like a movie. Quinn pushed the task onto her, and she pushed back. She loved that he crumpled first.

With Quinn on her mind, Ava headed for her car, but in moments, the reminder of Brandon's fatigue replaced the more pleasant thoughts. When she arrived home, her worry grew when she spotted him asleep on the couch, his backpack on the floor beside him. She studied his pallid color and beads of perspiration on his forehead. She placed her hand above his brow, then removed it, fearing she'd awaken him, and he'd be upset with her again. The battle between head and heart began as she sank into a chair and studied him, trying to decide what to do.

Ava settled on prayer.

In the silence, she gave her burden to the Lord. At least she tried to as she clung to Ross's advice. Bran knew his body. She needed to trust him. But would he admit feeling ill? That was her worry. He wanted to be well, but did he have the wisdom to recognize the return of Hodgkin's?

Her mother's instinct drilled a hole in her arguments. Let him be or ask questions? While she thought, he stirred. "Bran."

He shifted against the cushions without responding.

She pressed her lips together to stop herself from calling his name again. While she wrestled, Brandon opened his eyes and rolled on his side. "I think I have the flu or something."

She selected the appropriate question. "Is the flu going around?"

He closed his eyes and opened them with a nod. "Mike isn't feeling good, and Rick didn't come to school today."

Relief eased her anxiety. "I think you have a temperature." She rose. "I'll get the thermometer." He didn't protest, and she headed for the bathroom, praying it was only the flu. Night sweats was a symptom of Hodgkin's, not a fever. As she strode from the room, a sense of peace stilled her fear. God answered prayer in His own way. Today she'd experienced His grace.

Quinn stared at the flowerpot with a red bloom Ava clutched in her hand. "It's fine. Whatever you think."

"But I want your opinion."

"Ava, I don't know one flower from the other." His voice resounded in frustration, making him sorry he couldn't be as enthusiastic as she was.

"If you want a garden, maybe you should learn." Her eyes narrowed. "I seem to remember your giving advice about how to raise my son. I listened and learned."

"But I don't have to learn. I can hire people to do the thinking and the work for me." Her expression melted his heart. Without intending, he slipped his arm around her and gave her a hug. A rush of blood swept up his chest as he worked to keep a grip on his emotions. "I appreciate your trying to enlighten me. I suppose I'd be smart to know something about my garden."

Her questioning expression vanished as her eyes expanded, the hazel hue adorned by a glint of golden highlights in the afternoon sun.

Uncertain if the surprise stemmed from the embrace or his admission, he opened his mouth to apologize. But he closed it. Why make amends for his actions? He'd enjoyed every moment of the hug. Yet instead of fulfilling his yearning, it only aggravated his longing more. He'd felt whole for a fleeting moment.

Her expression and nearness sabotaged his lungs. He dragged in air as he forced his arm to lower. "What else do we need?" His voice sounded strange in his ears.

For a moment, she studied the shopping cart filled with flowers and plants they'd accumulated. Then she smiled. "I think this is it for now. I'm sure that makes you happy." She rested her hand on his arm as if nothing had happened.

But he knew it had. Even her smile enchanted him. "You mean we can go?"

Her hand slipped from his as she pointed to the cashier.

After paying, he loaded the SUV and pulled from the parking lot. Both fell into silence, and he questioned if her mind was as focused on the embrace as his was.

"Did I tell you about my latest scare?"

Her voice cut into his fantasy. "No. What happened?"

He listened as she relayed her worries about Brandon. His mind tore back to Sean and how healthy he'd been. Health and well-being had nothing to do with death. The realization set him on edge. Brandon had the chance to outlive Sean even though a serious disease had attacked his youthful body. Since he'd met Brandon, his prayer had been for the Lord to bless and heal him. Yet Quinn faced his envy, that Ava had her child with her. He sent a prayer heavenward that God forgive his thought. Ava deserved a healthy son. She'd already lost a husband.

Realizing that his mind had wandered, Quinn sought a response that fit the conversation. "You're sure it was the flu?"

She nodded, but he recognized the thread of doubt that lay beneath her expression. Did his face manifest the truth as hers did? He hoped not.

From Woodward Avenue, Quinn veered onto Lincoln Drive and then made a right onto York. As his home came into view, he admired the new roof shingles and the beige shutters and trim that gave the house a different look. He'd made good choices.

"It looks nice, Quinn. I think it makes your home even more stately."

Ava's choice of words surprised him. Stately? He'd never thought of his house in that light. His previous house would have seemed a mansion to her. "Thanks. I'm pleased."

"And I hope you'll be even more pleased when we finish the garden and the inside."

We. The word ruffled his senses. He'd been a me. An I. A single being. The connection unsettled him. He glanced at Ava as he backed into the driveway. "I'm sure I will."

Today he wrestled between his longing to feel whole and the knowledge that, if he faced his feelings for Ava, he would have to be open. She deserved to know everything about him, and he wasn't ready to admit what he'd kept hidden from most everyone. Only his brother knew the truth.

Ava opened the car door before he could round the SUV, and she met him at the back, her skin glowing in the afternoon sun. She'd worn light brown pants with a top the color of spring grass. She looked as fresh and dewy as the morning. Dragging his thoughts back to gardening, he raised the hatch. They pulled out potted plants and flats of flowers and toted them into the backyard.

Instead of placing the plants in one spot, Ava shifted them from one bed to another and then stood back, apparently devising a plan.

"Where do you want these?" He held up a flat of yellow flowers.

She studied them a moment, her rosy lips pressed together. "I knew when we bought them." She gave him an uneasy grin. "Now I can't remember."

"Let's bring them all back. You can look at the whole inventory."

She agreed, and after four trips, he grinned at the colorful display sitting on the lawn. "We have enough here for a park."

"I want to make it a showplace."

He eyed the ornate birdbath he'd neglected, admitting that the circular flower bed would be lovely if she had her way. "One more trip should do it."

Ava sent him a silly grin and stepped over the garden hose he'd attached to the water faucet, anticipating the new plants. As she did, her shoe caught beneath the rubber tubing and she catapulted forward. His pulse jarred as he charged to her side and clasped her in his arms as her knees buckled. He held her firm, her body braced against his. He drew her upward, reverting the fall. Their mouths an inch apart, his mind soared with temptation. Her lips, still parted with her outcry as she tumbled, appeared soft and yielding. Quinn gazed into her eyes the second time that day.

Her question seemed evident. He forced himself to steady her feet against the grass, one shoe caught beneath the garden hose. He latched on to the first diversion he could. "When I said the last trip, I didn't mean it literally."

A moment passed before her lips curved to a smile, and he studied her face, sensing a flash of disappointment. Or was it his own emotion he perceived?

Stunned by his uncontrolled emotion, he put distance between them and grasped her shoe. "Let's take a break." He tilted his head toward the house. "I'm thirsty and I'm sure you are, too." Without waiting for her response, he handed her the shoe and strode ahead, crossing the patio and holding open the family room door.

She stepped inside, dropped one shoe to the floor and slid off the other one. "I don't want to track grass on the carpet."

His heart in his mouth, he veered into the kitchen and she followed.

Before he invited her to sit, she'd opened the cabinet and brought down two tumblers. "Water?"

His chest constricted. Years had passed since anyone other than waitstaff had waited on him. He nodded and settled at the breakfast table, loving the familiarity he felt with her but struggling with it, as well.

While she filled the glasses with ice and water, he looked out the window, admiring the colors already brightening the lawn. When they were planted in the beds, he imagined the beauty they would bring to his landscape.

Before Ava handed him the drink, the telephone rang. He jumped as he often did when he heard the unexpected *brrring*. He rose and grabbed the wall phone before the third ring. His lawyer's voice caused him to wish he'd answered from his office. The attorney had interrupted another occasion with Ava. "Stephen, I have company. Could I—"

While he listened, Ava set the glasses on the table and slipped into the chair across from the seat he'd used.

"Are we short?" He watched her take a sip of the water. "Move the money then. That's not a problem. Yes, I know what I said." His back tensed as he talked in front of Ava. "I just like to know where it's going."

Though he wanted to cut the conversation short, Stephen gave him a rundown. Without lingering, he approved the shift of funds and said goodbye. When he returned to his chair and took a long swig of the icy drink, he leaned back, hoping to lead the conversation to their purchases, but Ava's expression stopped him cold.

"Business problems?" As she spewed the question, color rose to her cheeks. "I'm sorry, but I couldn't help but hear your side of the conversation."

His mind drew a blank. "Nothing serious."

Her heightened color lessened.

He tried to chuckle. "Businesses do all kinds of manipulating that wouldn't make sense to most people."

Concern etched her face and it was his turn to not understand. "Is there a problem?"

"No." She looked at the tabletop, but he knew she was troubled about something and he wished he could explain, but part of him didn't trust her to keep his secret quiet.

Ava waved her words away. "I always ask too many questions." She grinned, but it looked unconvincing. "It's your business—literally—and not mine."

He wanted to tell her about his involvement with Dreams Come True, but he'd set the anonymity clause as essential. The Lord said give humbly and he wanted no notoriety for his establishment of the funds. Ava had too many friends and she talked too much. He wasn't sure he ever wanted her to know because she might slip without meaning to. Instead of continuing the conversation, he managed a pleasant look and drained the glass of water. "Ready?"

The ice cubes tinkled as she lifted her tumbler and took a sip. Without responding, she rose, slipped into her shoes and opened the door.

Quinn wished he could redo their break and ignore the phone call, but it was too late. His hope rose that working with the flowers would encourage Ava to forget the conversation and enjoy the landscaping. He raised his shoulders, sensing she wouldn't be happy until he told her the whole truth, but until he knew her better he would keep quiet. The secret meant that much to him.

Chapter Seven

Ava stared out the living-room window, her mind sailing on stormy waters. One minute she'd been close to heaven and the next she'd sunk to the depths. Quinn's friendly hug had stirred her thoughts, but later she'd been caught up in the near kiss that she had no doubt would have happened if she'd encouraged it.

She'd wanted to with all her heart. Even though she'd tried to convince herself that romance would never darken her door, her heart hadn't been swayed. Quinn had appeared, and she'd been open to getting to know him.

Yet their conversation about the shifting funds had dug deep, brought out the keys and locked her door again. She didn't want to doubt him, but something on a gut level kept her from releasing an ominous feeling. He owned a business, and she supposed he could have various funds for purposes she didn't understand, so why did the fear rise and cause her to question him? Tom's face burst to her mind. She had to get over it. Tom had died. Quinn wasn't Tom.

Yes, Quinn held secrets that he clung to like gold. She sensed they were precious to him and letting go would reveal parts of him he didn't want known. She had to respect his privacy. She had secrets of her own. Ava shook her head at her own sick fears and crossed the room to gaze at the sky. A storm brewed in the distance. She'd heard the rumble of thunder as a zigzag of light flashed miles away.

Along with Quinn, Brandon's behavior bothered her. His fever had broken in a day, and he returned to school, and since then had come home to do homework or watch TV, but he wasn't himself. They hadn't had an argument in days. He hadn't asked to spend the night or hang out with his friends until today when he went with the guys to celebrate Mike's birthday. When Brandon stayed home, he went to bed early, and she didn't like his coloring.

She'd talked with him, or tried to, but he brushed off the couple of comments she'd made. Her only choice appeared to be starting an argument by demanding he see a doctor, and then what would happen to the trust she was trying to build with him?

Sinking back into the chair, Ava watched splashes of rain run down her windowpane. She thought of the flowers and hostas she'd planted at Quinn's. They would be watered today, and tomorrow they would grow in the warm sunshine. If only life were that easy, a few drops of rain and then growth, but today her nourishment had dried up. Life had held hope, a ray of sunlight, and now with Bran's health and her impossible feelings for Quinn, she'd become a desert plain.

Getting her concerns out of her mind seemed hopeless. She couldn't talk with Brandon, and she certainly couldn't discuss her quandary with Quinn. Both of them were her problems. Then she thought of Kelsey. The woman had a good mind, and she always seemed sensible. Ava headed for the telephone and dialed Kelsey's number, hoping she wasn't calling at their dinner hour.

When the ringing stopped, Kelsey answered the phone.

"Am I interrupting? This is Ava."

"Not one bit. In fact, I'm sitting here alone bored, and that's rare. Ross dropped Lucy and Peyton at Cooper's for the evening to play some games. He'll pick them up after the men's meeting at church tonight."

"I'd like to pick your brain if that's okay." Ava wanted to do more than pick, she wanted to plow into it for a revelation that would weaken her crazy thoughts.

"Is this about POSK?"

"No. It's personal." Her response sounded cryptic. Apparently Quinn's tacit manner had rubbed off on her.

"Want to come over? I baked some yummy cookies. They're made with miniature Snickers bars pressed in the middle."

"Conversation and cookies. I'd love to."

Kelsey was chuckling as she hung up.

Ava grabbed her handbag, locked the house and headed across town for Kelsey's. While she drove, she plotted her conversation, not wanting to say too much, yet telling her enough to make sense. The way she broached her concern would take thought.

Kelsey's grin greeted her when she opened the door, and Ava's tension faded. The scent of coffee hovered in the air as they approached the kitchen. Kelsey had set out a plate of cookies on the table, and she warmed to the old-fashioned coffee klatch.

"Have a seat while I pour the coffee."

Kelsey headed for the cabinet while Ava sank into the chair, having second thoughts about the conversation. She could talk about Brandon's situation, but her relationship with Quinn would best remain unspoken although she wasn't always good at that.

Kelsey set a cup in front of her, and then settled across the table. "Try a cookie."

Ava sipped the fragrant coffee, her mind a long distance away. When she finally reached for a cookie, Kelsey was studying her.

"Did you want to talk now?"

Her pulse skipped at Kelsey's question. The planned agenda crumbled as she searched for where to begin. "Part of it is Brandon. He hasn't been himself. Every day he talks about getting his learner's permit, and he hasn't mentioned it for a week or more."

Kelsey's expression remained blank, and Ava realized Lucy or Peyton weren't at the age to want to drive.

Organizing her thoughts, she started to explain her attempts to give him space, to trust him and to let him enjoy his health, but as she talked, Ava realized that the concern that permeated her thoughts was Quinn.

Kelsey shook her head. "Being tired is a symptom of Hodgkin's, isn't it?"

She nodded, but so were other things. "Quinn said that..." His name slipped out before she could stop it. "I meant to say Ross reminded me that Brandon knows his body and his health better than anyone."

"That's a sound statement."

Along with Kelsey's comment, Ava recognized a questioning look in her face. "Speaking of Quinn, are you still working for him?"

"The painter is almost finished and then I'll add artwork and a few toss pillows, whatever I need to do to turn his sterile decor into something warm and personal."

"Interesting." She lifted her cup and stared at the coffee. "He's changing. I noticed a difference at church."

"Changing in what way?"

"More outgoing." She shrugged. "It's just a feeling. He chatted with Ross a minute last Sunday. It might have been business. I'm not sure."

Business. The word flickered through her mind. "He's talking a little more, but he's still very secretive. By that I mean he keeps his personal life to himself."

Kelsey leaned closer, her look intense. "What are you worried about, Ava?"

The blunt question sounded like one of hers. "Can you keep this between us for now?"

Concern seeped into her eyes. "Sure."

"I like Quinn. A lot. And…I sense he cares about me, but we clash sometimes. He's so withdrawn about personal things. I know that his wife and son died in a car accident, and he left Grand Rapids where his business is—just walked away—and moved here. I wish I knew why he moved so far away from his business."

Kelsey frowned. "Does it really matter?"

The more she talked the more Ava realized she didn't make sense. "I guess not, but it seems strange. Is he running away from something? Or hiding?"

Kelsey's eyes widened. "What?"

Why had she opened her mouth? Kelsey knew nothing about Tom's problem. "Maybe I'm just suspicious. I've never told anyone, but Tom got involved in one of those pyramid schemes and we lost our savings. When I figured out what was happening, I put a stop to it, but I think the stress had been too much for him. When trust is shattered, it's difficult to put it back together. I suppose that's why I worry about my relationship with Brandon. I don't want to ruin the trust I'm trying to build with him." She'd never admitted her husband's mistake to anyone, and hearing it now sent ice down her limbs.

Kelsey reached across the table and touched her hand. "Keep an eye on the situation. That's all you can do. Hopefully Brandon is fine, but catching a health problem early is best, and as for Quinn, I think you're right. You're putting your husband's bad choice on him."

The warmth of her hand lifted as did her advice. "In my head, it sounds worse than when I say it here. I just worry about secrets. It's hard to trust someone when they have secrets." Again she thought of her own. "I appreciate your listening."

Kelsey withdrew her hand to lift the cookie plate. "Anytime. Now enjoy the dessert while I warm up your coffee."

"Is that you?" Ava leaned out of the utility room into the kitchen.

"No, I'm a burglar." Bran's voice, though lighthearted, held a hint of irritation.

Ava lowered the lid on the washing machine and followed Brandon's footsteps into the living room. He'd grabbed the TV remote and sprawled on the sofa. She stood in the archway and studied him. "Are you okay?"

"Why do you keep asking that, Mom? I'm fine."

"I'm worried about you." She clamped her teeth together, wishing she'd rephrased her statement. "The flu took more out of you than I would expect."

"Maybe it was the plague. The black plague." He flipped to another channel.

Ava wandered to his side and sat on the edge of the sofa near his feet. "Do you think we should call the oncologist and—"

His fist smacked the cushion. "I thought you were going to trust me."

Ava bolted up. "I do, but—"

Brandon slipped his feet to the floor and pressed his forehead into his hands. "I'm tired of doctors and hospitals and tests. That's what makes me tired."

She backed away and sank into an easy chair. "So am I, Bran. Nothing makes me happier than to see you healthy and happy."

He studied her face a moment. "I know you're trying to be a good mother. I know what Hodgkin's feels like. This is different. My throat has been sore, and I'm more tired than usual. You know I have a lot of pressure at school. I have a big English project to finish and the stupid chemistry is driving me nuts. I only got a B on that test. I don't want my GPA to drop."

Weighing his comments, Ava's tension lessened. Worry could do a lot of things, and maybe the flu had hung on longer than usual. "Okay, I understand." She bit her top lip, deciding if she should take a chance. "Can we do this? Let's wait another week or so, and if you're still dragging like you are, then maybe we should make an appointment."

Brandon shook his head. "You never give up. Okay. Another week or so." He shifted and stretched out on the sofa. "I haven't missed school. I'm eating okay."

But not the same as usual, though he would deny it. "You haven't asked about a learner's permit in a week."

His blink let her know her comment surprised him. He shrugged. "I've been preoccupied with school." As if he'd gained new life, he propped his head up. "And I don't see you as much, either, Mom. You've been hanging out with the dude who ran into you."

Her pulse skipped. "You know his name." She tossed off the remark, hoping to cover the shock she'd felt with his dig. Heat rose on her chest. "I'm working for him. I'm earning money."

"Doing what?" A look of disbelief washed over his face. "Housekeeping? You already have a job at the school."

"Quinn is renovating his home, and I'm doing some interior decorating for him…and some landscaping." Resentment engulfed her. She didn't like his attitude or his disrespect. "I have talents, Brandon, although you maybe don't recognize them. I would have loved a career in interior design, but life doesn't always go as we plan."

"I suppose I'm the problem. You had me."

His biting comment knocked the wind from her lungs. "You were planned. I wanted you and so did your father."

He shrugged again and hit the remote. Audience laughter broke the silence that hung between them.

The tension had to end, but what she could say escaped her. "I'm sorry that you feel neglected, Bran. It's extra income, and we need it. I usually work there when I know you're busy. I've always been here for you. Always. I didn't know you resented my friendship with Quinn that much."

Instead of blasting her with a bitter comment, Brandon closed his eyes and lowered his head. "I'm sorry."

"Thank you. That means a lot to me." She melted with his hangdog look. "If my friendship with Quinn bothers you, then let me know. I'm enjoying the work. I've done what I can afford to do here, and I thought I made a cozy home for us."

"Mom. The house is great. I guess I feel cornered, and I just lashed out. You're right. You've always been here for me." A faint grin curved his mouth. "Sometimes more than I want."

His expression made her smile. "I know that, too." She rose and walked to his side. "I love you, Bran. You've been my life." She leaned over and kissed his cheek.

He gave a nod. "I love you, too."

As she walked away, her last words rang in her head. *You've been my life.* He had been, and recently, she longed for a life of her own. And that's exactly what Quinn needed, too.

Quinn stood back and studied Ava surveying the paint job in the living room. The forest-green with white trim had jarred his mind when she mentioned it, but he'd given her the go-ahead to do the job, and he didn't want to start nixing her ideas. Now he realized she'd been correct.

She turned to face him. "What do you think?"

He chuckled, a rare feeling for him until Ava had come along. "It's stunning." He stepped closer, drawn to her even more since the last time they'd been together when he'd saved her from the fall. He hadn't been the same since. His lips ached to touch hers, and he longed to feel her in his arms again.

"Really?" She eyed him, tilting her head with disbelief.

"I admit I wasn't sure when you suggested it, but now, I like it. The color is vibrant and yet calming, like a walk in the woods."

"Good. That's what I wanted." She held her hand up for a high five, and he smacked his palm to hers. Her hands felt small and fragile.

"And the kitchen is even more amazing."

Her face brightened. "You like it."

"It's like sunshine on the Grand Canyon."

She giggled like a schoolgirl. "I never thought you'd be poetic."

She knew so little about him, but he only grinned back. "So where do we go from here?"

His question spun in her mind.

"Are we done with the inside, I mean?"

The color came back to her face. "I already told you. This is only the beginning. You want me to bring this place to life so it will need wall decor, rugs, pillows, art pieces. That means shopping."

He tried not to turn up his nose. "I remember."

"But here's another thought." She pointed toward the staircase. "You have lots of boxes stored upstairs. I suppose you have some things there that I can use rather than buy everything new. Would you go through them with me?"

His stomach churned. "I have no interest in plowing through all of that."

A frown settled on her face. "But you haven't thrown it away so it must have meant something to you. Why not use a few things that will add meaning to the rooms?"

He squirmed with her suggestion, but maybe she had a point. "You're welcome to look through it if you really want to."

She gave him a sideways look as if weighing his suggestion. "Okay, but you'll accept what I choose?"

Did he have a choice? He nodded. "It's a deal. If it will keep me from shopping, then—"

A smile broke free from her thoughtful expression. "I didn't say that."

Quinn laughed. It felt amazing. "Is that what you want to do now?" He motioned toward the staircase.

"Not today. I'll need time for that." Her smile vanished back to her earlier reflection. "That reminds me of something we should talk about."

The word *talk* bombarded his confidence. He'd thought their day might move along without incident, but Ava's talk concerned him. More probing questions. More asking details. More topics he couldn't handle. He pulled his head from the fragments of his conclusion. "Talk about what?"

"Brandon and me."

The firing squad backed away. "Problems?" He motioned for her to sit.

She eyed the room and settled onto the sofa where she always sat when she was in the living room. "Don't misconstrue what I'm saying, please."

His back stiffened.

"I think Brandon is jealous of you…but not exactly you. I think it's the time I spend with you. He snapped a comment at me a couple days ago, but later apologized so I let it go. We came to a kind of resolution, but from his dig—and that's how I saw it—he wanted to know why I was spending so much time with you."

Quinn listened while she told him about calling her his housekeeper, the end of the school year excuse and his lack of reference to the learner's permit.

"Is he sleeping all the time?"

"Much more than usual, and he said he has a sore throat and blames the flu that was going around, but—"

"You're still worried."

She nodded. "We agreed on calling his oncologist if he's not feeling well in a week."

"He agreed?"

She lifted one shoulder. "But his heart wasn't in it. I've tried to give him room to make decisions, but now I wonder if I should back off coming here so much."

His stomach took a nosedive. "He knows this is a job, right?"

"I'm not sure he believes it, but yes."

Quinn didn't believe it, either. At least not from his perspective. His pulse skipped when he spoke to her on the phone. He'd reverted back to his early years when he discovered girls or when he'd met Lydia. No matter what he felt, he didn't want to cause a rift. "If you need to leave, I understand." It took all he had to say those words.

"He's out with friends tonight. I'm fine."

He tried to think of possible solutions. "How about the landscaping? Can we look outside and decide what else you want for the garden? I was thinking I could hire Brandon to help, and he could even earn spending money."

She studied his face as if trying to decide if he were joking. "You're serious."

He nodded.

"I wonder if Bran would agree. The circular birdbath bed needs more work, and you have a wonderful sunny area perfect for roses. They make beautiful floral arrangements for the house."

His spirit lifted as he watched enthusiasm return to her face. "Let's take a look." He rose and strode through the family room to the patio doorway. But his mind wasn't on landscaping or floral arrangements. His awareness tangled in the most lovely thing in his home. Ava. Yet along with Ava stress and worries marched along. Nothing new to him. What was new to him set his pulse on a gallop. His feelings for Ava grew by the minute, and he had no idea where it would lead. And now he had Brandon to worry about, too.

Chapter Eight

When the last hymn ended, Ava replaced the hymnbook and scanned the congregation, looking for Quinn. She wanted to surprise him. Only Kelsey knew she'd planned to attend the worship service, and her greatest joy was Brandon had agreed to come with her.

Kelsey stepped beside her and opened her arms. "Great to see you here." She extended her hand to Brandon. "And you, too. I hope you enjoyed the service."

Brandon grinned. "I liked the band."

Though Ava cringed at his comment, Kelsey chuckled. "Whatever brings you here, the Lord is pleased."

Brandon's grin faded as he looked past Kelsey, and Ava suspected who he saw. She looked in the same direction and observed Quinn making his way through the worshipers.

"This is a pleasant surprise." He noticed Brandon and did a double take. "Nice to see you both."

"I thought we might surprise you." Brandon's expression made her wish she'd kept that comment to herself. She'd hear about it later.

Kelsey touched her arm. "Will you stay for coffee?"

Ava gave Brandon a questioning look. "Is it okay?"

"They have treats." Kelsey motioned toward the fellow-ship hall.

Brandon nodded. "I guess so."

Knowing food could lure most teenagers, Ava sent Kelsey a look of thanks before she returned to Ross who was talking to a man.

Ava eyed Quinn. "Are you staying?" She held her breath.

"I'll join you if you don't mind." He turned to Brandon. "I have an offer for this young man anyway."

Hearing him agree excited Ava, but Brandon's reaction set her on edge. A scowl emerged on his face. "What kind of an offer?"

"One that involves a job." He rested his hand on Brandon's shoulder. "For money."

Surprising her, Quinn steered Brandon away from the group, and they walked together toward the fellowship hall. She followed at a distance with Kelsey calling her to join them. When Ava reached her, Kelsey gave a toss of her head. "Interesting that Quinn's talking to Brandon, isn't it?"

Ava explained the job and Quinn's two-fold motivation. "Quinn asked me what I thought before he initiated this."

"It's great for him to get involved. I'm sure Brandon can use a man's attention." She gave Ava a one-armed hug. "I don't mean that you're not a great mother."

"Don't apologize. I'm with you. He has few male influences except for a couple of teachers and his friends' fathers. But those aren't really relationships. Quinn could be one."

Kelsey sent her a knowing look. "And you were worried about him." She gave her head a shake. "I'm confident he's a good man." She shrugged. "I hope I'm right."

Ava hoped, too, because she'd agreed to Quinn's plan. If he and Bran got to know each other, Bran would be more open to their friendship.

When one of the church ladies stopped Kelsey, Ava moved

along, her mind reverting to the worship service. She was glad she'd come. The music uplifted her, and the sermon on trust hit home. Her trust problem began with her husband's secret involvement with the bad investment, and now she'd almost lost it with Brandon, but the lesson reminded her that by trusting God, faith and hope were also a gift from Him. She'd rarely addressed hope with any possibility. She'd hung it on a hook in the recesses of her mind along with her faith. Today her hope tiptoed back into the light.

Quinn gave her a wave as she entered the fellowship hall. She grabbed a coffee and found a chair beside him. Noticing their grins, she sensed that he and Brandon had come to an agreement. She hoped Brandon would tell her what happened when they were alone.

Ross stopped by and chatted a moment with Quinn, and Ross appeared pleased that Quinn had stayed for coffee. He sent Ava a suspecting grin, the insinuation she could no longer deny. The relationship with Quinn had blossomed beyond friendship, but admitting it aloud could change the natural course of their journey and add to her vulnerability since she couldn't speak for Quinn's feelings.

When Quinn rose to leave, Ava beckoned to Brandon, and they joined him outside.

Quinn paused at her car and opened her door. "I told Brandon about the flowers we bought yesterday, and he wants to start planting them today. Will that work for you?"

Her heartbeat skittered along her veins. "Sure, if Bran's willing." She bent down and looked at him in the passenger seat as she gave him a smile. Though he didn't smile back, he didn't frown, either. That was a good sign.

Before she climbed in, Quinn touched her shoulder, his eyes telling her the talk went well. "See you later."

She gave a nod and slipped inside, her faith growing each moment. Worship, prayer, faith and hope. She longed to add love to the list.

* * *

Quinn stood back, watching the dynamics between Ava and Brandon. Ava's attempts to give Brandon the reins pleased him. As always, he admired Ava's desire to change her life. He only wished he could bend as easily. But then maybe he had. Getting involved with her son meant taking a giant step away from his personal grief to moving forward. He could thank Ava for that. The day she plowed into him she'd opened doors he'd thought were nailed closed.

While Brandon worked on one side of the circular flower bed, Ava knelt on a rubber pad setting wave petunias into the soil. Quinn didn't know one petunia from the other, but Ava insisted they would spread. She'd run home after church and slipped on blue capris and a blue-and-pink-print top, the same tint as the petunias.

Quinn lowered the flat of flowers, letting her grab another container while he admired her easy smile and look of contentment. He suspected he looked the same. Connecting with her and Brandon meant more to him than he wanted to admit.

Knowing he had another job to do, Quinn set the flat beside Ava and grabbed the trimmers, attacking another shrub that wanted to be a tree. Three years of letting things grow had turned an attractive garden into a jungle. Little by little the landscape took shape, and he had Ava to thank.

She rose and wiped perspiration from her forehead. "What do you think?"

"I think you need a break." He stepped close and eyed the rosy shade on her arms and nose. "I think you're getting a burn."

Her gaze lowered to her arms. "I think you're right." She walked to the umbrella table and sipped the iced tea he'd offered them. Brandon had accepted a can of pop.

The boy rent his heart. Though strong in appearance,

Quinn noted the weakness that Ava had brought to his attention, and concern edged out the hope that she was wrong.

Ava ambled to his side, pulling off her garden gloves. "Would you mind if I take a break inside? Maybe I could tackle the attic boxes for a while and get out of the sun."

His stomach constricted, and he wished she'd never seen the cartons full of memories. Though he no longer remembered what lay inside, he saw them as wounds covered with bandages. Opening them could make him bleed again.

Her eager face forced him to give a nod. "It might be warm up there."

"Not as hot as it is here." She gave a wave and strode toward the patio doorway into the family room.

Opportunity to spend time alone with Brandon provided the most positive part of her decision to rummage the attic. He sidled closer with the rabbiting spade perfect for planting bulbs or annuals. "How about if I dig the holes and you put in the plants."

Brandon tilted his head upward and nodded, taking Quinn aback. His pale face seemed tinted yellow—not a golden glow from the sun but a sickly shade that concerned him. As he pushed the narrow shovel into the soil, he struggled how to broach the subject.

Brandon grasped a plant, set it inside the hole and pushed the dirt around the roots. When he paused a moment, Quinn took advantage.

"I think you need a break, too." He dropped the shovel onto the grass and beckoned for Brandon to rise.

The boy pushed himself up, exhaustion written on his face.

"I think that flu you had isn't gone yet. Your color isn't good, Brandon."

Brandon pulled off his work gloves and dropped them beside the flat of flowers. "You sound like my mom."

Quinn chuckled as he rested his hand on the boy's shoulder. "I appreciate your hard work, but I'm concerned, too."

Brandon shot him a look that he expected his mother witnessed often.

"You'd like me to butt out, I suspect, but here's the thing. Your mom says great things about you, and I know she's trying to let you be an adult. That's hard for moms."

"You can say that again."

Beneath the comment, Brandon let a faint grin slip to his mouth.

"And she gives you credit for being bright and capable. I can see why. Beside your good grades, you're a hard worker. That's commendable."

Though Brandon tried to hide his reaction, Quinn saw the boy was pleased. "Even without a dad in your life now, you're trying to be the man in your family, but men need to face facts, too. Sometimes we get sick, and the most important thing is to get better."

His shoulders drooping, the boy lifted his gaze. "She told you I agreed to see a doctor if I don't feel better?"

"She did, but I think it's time. I have more jobs for you, but I'd rather you get your strength back first." He gave Brandon's shoulder a pat. "Your mom will be relieved and I think you will, too."

He lowered his head, and Quinn could almost hear his mind ticking. "My throat's still sore." He mumbled a list of complaints. "I'm tired all the time, too."

Silence stretched too long while Brandon stared at the ground.

"Brandon?"

"Okay. I'll tell her."

"Great. That's a wise decision." An idea niggled in his mind, one he'd tried to stop, the memory so fresh as to what happened to Sean, but it was time to let go. "I know you want to get your learner's permit. Are your classes and on-road instruction completed?"

A sigh emphasized his defeated look. "It will be in three more weeks."

A knot tightened in Quinn's chest. "How about this. When you have a clean bill of health, I'll be on your side."

A smile filled Brandon's face, one Quinn had never seen before. "You will?"

"Promise." Quinn longed to embrace the boy as memories flooded over him. Why hadn't he demonstrated his support to his son more when he could? The moot question hung on the air. Because he'd been lost in his business. Now he'd taken the tragedy and learned from it. Today he chalked up a major difference in his life, having found another example of personal growth that freed him. The emptiness he'd lived with ebbed for the first time in three years.

Ava opened an upstairs bedroom window where she'd spotted some of the stored boxes. A waft of air swept in, whisking away the closed-up smell permeating the room. Dust bunnies gathered beneath pieces of unused furniture, and a few had huddled in the corner as if trying to escape a broom, but she guessed the upstairs hadn't seen a broom for a long time. Quinn let her know he used the space for nothing more than storage.

The breeze drew her back to the window, and when she looked down, she saw Quinn and Brandon working together. Her chest tightened as she watched them. Man to man. She ached thinking of a teen boy with questions and experiences best shared with a dad.

Her eyes on Quinn, she noted he'd dressed in jeans. That was a first. She didn't think he owned them. He looked good, more relaxed and unrestrained. She wished she could be a field mouse listening in.

Forcing herself to turn away from the view, Ava opened one of the boxes and looked inside. Decorative pillows— stripes, abstract shades of brown, and two lovely pillows with a byzantine motif. The maze pattern in antique gold and citron tones would look perfect in the living room with the green leaf patterns in the sofa.

After setting four pillows on one of the stored chairs, she opened another carton. Newspaper hid the items inside. She noted the date: June 11, 2009, a few days before her birthday. Beneath the wrapping, Ava spotted a crystal sphere seated on a hand-carved birch pedestal, a must to use somewhere. In another box, she found four black-and-white cloud prints in black frames with white matting, a beautiful addition to the decor and a reflection of Quinn's love for nature.

When she opened another carton, her heart skipped. Photograph albums. Family pictures, she was sure. She lifted one out, settled on the floor, using a box as a prop for her back, and opened the cover. Quinn, a few years younger, looked at the camera, a smile lighting his face, and beside him an attractive woman with blond hair and a boy about eleven—maybe twelve—grinned at the photographer. The tightness in her throat caused her to lower her head and close her eyes as moisture beaded her lashes. In one fleeting moment, these two were gone, leaving Quinn empty and alone. She brushed away the tears with the back of her hand, then reached down with trembling fingers to turn the page.

"Ava?"

Quinn. She slammed the album closed, dropped it back in the carton and rose. "Coming." She picked up the framed mirror and checked her face. The tears left no telltale sign. She placed it back on a box top and headed to the stairs.

At the bottom, Quinn looked at her, an unsettling expression on his face. Her stomach knotted, fearing something happened between him and Brandon. "Problem?"

"No." He gave a fleeting tilt of his head toward the living room. "I'm going to rustle up something to eat, and—"

"You?" She appreciated the opportunity to lighten the mood. "Cereal or a frozen dinner?"

"Maybe I'll surprise you." When she reached the bottom step, he leaned close to her ear. "And so will this. Brandon wants to talk with you."

Her eyes captured his, but he only nodded toward the archway. She straightened to her full five feet six inches and strode past Quinn, her heart in her throat.

Ava eyed the wall clock in the sterile-colored examining room. Bran sat beside her, flipping through a sports magazine he'd found in a rack, waiting for the oncologist to open the door.

Though grateful Quinn had motivated Brandon to see the oncologist, Ava stung from the notion that her son would rather listen to a stranger's advice than his mother's. The grudging thought faded when she pictured Bran and Quinn talking together in the flower garden. For once, Bran's face had looked up at Quinn with interest and his body language reflected the same. They had talked, and he'd listened. She should be more than grateful.

A tap on the door alerted them, and the door pushed open as Dr. Franklin stepped inside and closed the door. He sat on the stool and rolled closer to Brandon, asking the questions they expected.

"I've been feeling sick for a week or so." Brandon glanced at her, asking if she'd back him up.

But she couldn't. "It's been over two weeks. He insisted he was fine, but he hasn't improved. He still has the sore throat, and I don't like his coloring."

Brandon shot her the familiar thanks-for-nothing look. Today she didn't care. Her son needed medical attention.

The doctor rose, tilted Brandon's head upward and looked into his eyes. A frown fluttered across his face, and he lifted Brandon's hand a moment and studied it. "You have jaundice. Let me look at your throat." He grabbed a tongue depressor and peered inside. He shook his head.

Ava's heart skipped a beat. "How bad is he?"

Dr. Franklin settled back on the stool and flipped through Brandon's records. "Jaundice is a symptom, not a disorder, and the throat could be strep. But most important, with your history, Brandon, we need to know what's going on here." He motioned for Brandon to stretch out on the examining table. "Let's check your lymph nodes."

When Ava realized he was checking for swelling, she excused herself and stepped into the hall. Rather than wait by the door, she headed to the waiting room for a cup of coffee.

The acrid scent gave her pause when she poured the black liquid. She took it anyway and sank into a chair, her mind piling with questions. Jaundice. How had she missed it? She'd noticed his coloring was different days ago, but then, her thoughts weren't totally on Bran. Quinn and the decorating project had filled her mind and wouldn't budge. She lowered her head, unable to grasp the hold Quinn had on her.

She couldn't blame him. He'd given her a casual hug and caught her when she tripped, but the look in his eyes had whispered to her. Being alone for the past years, she'd carried the burden of Bran's illness, and being the only income-earner in the house hadn't left her with time or inclination to pursue romance. She didn't know if she had the energy now. But her emotions drove her forward without reason.

No, the feelings weren't without reason. Quinn made her feel like a woman. She hadn't felt like anything except Brandon's mother for years. And Quinn was the most thoughtful… and surprising man she'd ever known.

Sunday's surprise hung in her mind. By his admission, Quinn never cooked, but the last time she'd been there—the day Brandon agreed to see the oncologist—Quinn had prepared a meal for them. And not just any meal. He'd grilled steaks, tender and delicious, and served them along with microwave-baked potatoes and frozen mixed vegetables. She avoided teasing him about being frozen. The tender, delicious steak made up for the frozen veggies.

Ava took a sip of the thick coffee and drew back. Bad choice. She eyed the waiting-room clock and rose, disposing of the cup on her way back to the examining room. The truth mounted as she approached the door. If she'd been more persistent rather than letting it slip for the sake of making Brandon happy, he'd have gotten to the office sooner. She sent up a prayer for good news and tapped on the door.

Bran's "it's okay" gave her confidence to enter. She stood beside the door studying him before catching the doctor's eye. "What do you think?"

Dr. Franklin pulled his eyes from the pile of records he'd been perusing. "Swollen lymph glands, sore throat, jaundice and fatigue is a sign for mononucleosis."

"Mono? But how would that happen?" She'd heard it called the kissing disease, but Bran didn't have a girlfriend. At least, she didn't think so. She eyed Brandon.

He gave a shrug. "I don't know, Mom."

"It's very contagious, Mrs. Darnell. It's caused by Epstein-Barr virus which is contagious by way of saliva. That can happen through kissing, or sharing food or drinks with someone." Dr. Franklin gave Brandon a faint grin. "I suppose you've done one or two of those things. Teenagers often do."

Brandon gave a guilty nod.

The physician gave his leg a pat and beckoned him to sit up. "I'll have a full blood count done along with a monospot test to confirm the mono and rule out Hodgkin's, but I may decide to schedule an MRI. We'll see what the blood work shows, but with Hodgkin's, I don't want to take chances."

Ava's hopes rose. "You think it's only mono?"

The oncologist stood. "I think so, but we want to make sure." He turned to Brandon. "You wait here, and I'll send in a medical assistant to draw your blood." He opened the door and closed it behind him.

"Mono." Brandon shook his head. "Bill's brother had mono a few weeks ago."

"And you were at their house."

He lowered his head as he nodded.

Instead of commenting, Ava let it go. He didn't know Bill's brother was ill, and calling him up on the situation would only cause a ruckus. "I'm glad we came, aren't you?"

He lifted his head with another nod.

"At least we'll know what it is, and what we can do to make you better."

Brandon settled back in the chair he'd vacated, and Ava didn't persist in conversation. Grateful that mono might be all it was, she dwelled on the positive. Her fears had grown, as they always did, expecting the worst, but God answered her prayers.

The melody of her cell phone broke the silence. She pulled it from her handbag. Quinn's phone number brightened the window.

Quinn's voice sounded deep on the phone—a rich tone that rolled through her. "Are you still there?"

"We are. He's having blood work done. They think it's mono."

He blew a swish of air into the phone. "That's great news."

She hoped it was, explaining the type of blood work and the possible MRI. "Dr. Franklin sounded fairly certain so it is good news."

"Tell Brandon I've sent up some prayers and I'm happy to hear they were answered."

"Thanks." Quinn's faith shone stronger than hers could ever be. He'd gone through the deaths of his entire family and remained a staunch believer. Could she have done that?

"I have to go to Grand Rapids for a couple of days."

The joy in her heart dimmed. "Business?"

"Yes. My brother and I have some situations to handle, but I'd like to give you the keys to the house so if you want to work while I'm gone you can. I don't suppose Brandon will continue right now, but—"

"We'll see what the doctor says about that." Her chest constricted as she thought of his trust. "You don't mind my being in your house without you?"

"Why would I? You're not a thief, are you?" He chuckled.

She managed a laugh, but her inklings about Quinn's being involved in something shady raised her guilt. She longed to trust him.

"I'll bring over the keys tonight if that's all right. I'm leaving early in the morning."

"I'll be there."

When he disconnected, Ava dropped the cell phone into her handbag and leaned back, her mind twisting around many things—Brandon's blood tests, her relationship with Quinn and her uncertainty.

She despised the muddied emotions.

Chapter Nine

$\mathcal{A}$va filled her glass with ice water and slipped onto the kitchen chair. She felt odd working in Quinn's home with him in Grand Rapids, but he'd been comfortable with it, so she accepted his offer. Besides the key, he'd given her and Brandon a generous check for their work. Though happy for Brandon, she winced taking the money. She'd received more joy from having the opportunity to explore his gorgeous home and gardens, and her contribution to his decor had been pure pleasure.

Brandon had tried to convince her to let him finish the planting, but she'd watered the flowers, still in pots, and insisted he follow the doctor's orders and rest. The school had cooperated with his need to stay home for a few days, and he'd been allowed to alter his final class projects. Even a couple of his teachers had dropped by the office to let her know how happy they were it was only mono and not a relapse of his Hodgkin's lymphoma. She'd been grateful for everyone's concern.

Able to relax now that she knew what ailed Brandon, Ava had delved into her work. She set out items for Quinn to approve, many lovely pieces to add to the decor and a couple of things she worried Quinn might not appreciate. He'd made it clear that his past life was private, but she believed strongly that he needed to accept it so that he could move on. She'd taken some of the photos from the album to use in the decor, but when she thought about the possible repercussions, she closed her eyes and prayed.

Anxious for Quinn to see what she'd done, Ava wandered into the living room, admiring the additions. The pillows were perfect and the splash of antique gold and citron added a color contrast to the forest-green and white walls. She'd found an oil painting of an old house, the roof touched by the gold of a sunset, surrounded by a field of yellow daisies. She'd hung the artwork over the fireplace mantel, the perfect location for a Belleck vase in a sandwave pattern and a fluted saffron-hued vase with a white Byzantine design. Striking.

She took a sip of the water she carried as she ambled through the archway and stood in his office doorway. With only one window, she'd had the room painted in a rich cream to enhance the light with one wall in saddle-brown for a splash of color. The room needed her handiwork, but she wanted Quinn's input. She had added one item to his credenza, the crystal sphere seated on the hand-carved birch pedestal.

She set her water on the edge of the desk and crossed the room to adjust the crystal. When she did, a prism of light fell across the beige carpet in a rainbow of color. God's rainbow. Her heart lifted. She backed toward the desk and reached for her glass of water. Instead, she struck the side, and the water sloshed onto the desk. In panic, she grabbed the stack of letters piled on the desk, swooping them away as some fell to the floor.

Putting the water there had been stupid. She knelt, grasping the sheets of paper into a pile. As she did, her focus fell on a letter with his attorney's signature at the bottom. Her heart stopped as she slipped it into the pile.

Three words in the body of the letter burned into her vision. *Dreams Come True.*

Her pulse hammering, she set the letters to the side away from the water spill and backed away into the doorjamb.

"Careful."

Her heart nose-dived to her stomach as she spun around. "Quinn. What are you doing here?"

He grinned. "I live here. Have you forgotten?"

Her skin burned as she struggled to regain her decorum. "I wasn't expecting you today." Her guilt sent a neon sign to her forehead, and she was certain he'd suspect she'd been snooping.

"We finished early." He gazed at her a moment, concern etching his face. "Is something wrong? Is it Brandon's blood work?"

"No, you scared me. I'm sorry I was careless and sloshed water on your desk."

"It's only water. Nothing's hurt." He rested her hand on her shoulder. "Brandon's okay?"

"Yes, I heard from Dr. Franklin. The blood work and monospot test indicated mono and no need for an MRI. So that was a relief." His genuine caring expression helped to chase away her guilt. She'd gone into his office to admire the room. Seeing the letter had been an accident. She gestured through the doorway. "I hope you like the color of your office as much as I do."

He strode to the doorway and leaned inside. "The crystal globe looks good there. It catches the sun."

Guilt taking over her senses, she backed farther from the office. "I need a paper towel to clean up the spill."

"Looks like you moved the stack of letters." He waved her words away. "No damage." He strode past her and veered through the family room into the kitchen.

She followed, heading for the paper towel roll, but Quinn

caught her arm, and drew her closer to him. "I missed being here." His eyes searched hers. "And I missed seeing you."

The temperature rose. Her cheeks burned as she gazed at him not knowing if she should say thank-you or toss out a lighthearted comment. Before she could move, he slipped his arm around her.

"What's Brandon up to now?"

The change in topic caught her off guard. "Resting. No school until next week, but he's fine."

"I'm relieved." He brushed her cheek with his index finger.

His eyes searched hers, making her uncomfortable. She didn't understand the touch or his embrace. Her mind spun. "Did you see the living room?"

His head bolted back as if she'd surprised him. "No. I came in through the garage."

She struggled for breath. "Come take a look." She beckoned to him, trying to keep her hands from shaking. She needed to get a grip.

He followed her lead, and when he reached the archway, he stopped, his gaze sweeping the room. "Wow! That makes a difference."

"Do you like it?"

"I do, but…"

She hung on his voice waiting for him to finish the sentence, but he only gazed at her. "But what?"

Quinn drew closer and slipped both arms around her. "But I like you more."

Ava sensed it coming before it happened. His eyes grew heavy as his mouth sought hers. Overwhelmed with surprise, she sank into his arms, her pulse bombarding her ears. Without knowing, she had slipped her arms around his back, his muscles flexing as he raised his arm and ran his fingers through her hair.

Dazed, she let it happen, her secret longing seeped into reality while his lips moved on hers as soft and gentle as a kitten's purr. When he drew back, she caught her breath, her mind unable to form a sentence, but sensing she should say something.

"I've wanted to do this for a long time, Ava." His whisper brushed her cheek and tangled in her hair.

She found her voice. "And I've wanted you to…even though I'm not sure it's wise."

His body jerked as he searched her eyes. "Why do you say that?"

"We're new friends, Quinn. I have a son who needs my attention, and you have things you need to deal with." She'd hit home with her comment. His face drained of color.

"But it doesn't diminish my feelings for you and Brandon."

"But until you deal with it, Quinn, you can't give your all to anyone. I'm not jealous of that. I understand, but I think you have some work to do."

His arms slipped from her, but he captured her hand in his. "I admire you more than I can say, and I take what you've said to heart. We both have changes to make, and we're both making strides."

He'd included her, and she supposed he was right. "You're talking about me and Brandon?"

"You've made progress."

A sad feeling washed over her. "I know I still have work."

"Then let's work on things together."

Together. The word drifted in the air like a feather. She could only nod.

Quinn strode into fellowship hall wondering if he'd missed Ava. When he arrived for the worship service, he'd tried to be discreet as he searched the faces of the congregation, but he hadn't seen her. Though he told himself he was surprised at his reaction, today he admitted when Ava wasn't there, he missed her. Too much.

But now he worried he'd made a mistake. The impromptu

kiss surprised him as much as her. He'd longed to embrace her, to feel her lips on his, but until the moment when he looked into her eyes, the reality was far from him. The only woman he'd kissed for many years had been Lydia, but Thursday's kiss had touched him beyond his expectation. She'd burrowed into his heart since he met her and the kiss had unleashed his emotions.

With Ava's absence, his first concern was Brandon. His second was the kiss. Had she reconsidered it and wanted to avoid him? The concern prickled up his spine. Pouring a cup of coffee, he scanned the crowd and spotted Ross. The worrying idea he'd been considering rose again and he wanted to toss it around with someone else before he spoke with Ava. He gave Ross a wave and ambled toward him.

Ross extended his hand, and Quinn grasped it with a firm shake. A crooked grin grew on Ross's face. "How are things going with Ava?"

Quinn's heart kicked, and he swallowed.

"Are you happy with her work? She seems to enjoy it."

His discomfort fading, Quinn managed a smile. "I'm very happy. She's done amazing things with paint selections and some of the old junk I had stored upstairs." Stretching the truth, he experienced a guilty nudge. He could have admitted Ava had dragged out pieces of his old life and made him face it. She'd said it was time, and it was.

"Good." Ross gave his back a light smack. "With your endorsement, I can recommend Ava to some of our customers looking for a decorator. That's not our bag, but if I can offer some help in that way, it pleases our clients, and in the long run we get more jobs from their recommendation."

"Word of mouth is the best promotion my company can get." Hearing the reference to his company surprised Quinn. He'd kept that as closed off as he did himself. Weight lifted from his shoulders. Talking about his life had become easier.

Ross motioned to two vacant chairs, and Quinn sank into

one as Kelsey approached with a cream-filled doughnut. His stomach gnawed.

"Quinn." She sat her food on the table and extended her hand.

He rose and grasped it before sliding the chair toward her, but Ross had already grabbed another. He sank back into the chair, noticing the look on her face. He knew Ava talked with her, but he didn't know how much Kelsey knew. The kiss came to mind, and heat edged up his chest, making him uneasy.

Kelsey searched his eyes. "You've gotten to know Brandon pretty well, I understand."

Pin prickles rolled up his back, but he managed to give a casual shrug. "Trying to be supportive, I guess."

She pinched off a piece of the doughnut. "Ava approves, I'm sure."

As she dropped the sweet into her mouth, he noticed a little grin, and he steered away from talking about his relationship with Ava. "I've been weighing the idea of having a concrete slab poured behind my garage and attaching a basketball hoop to the garage wall." When he spotted their expressions, he wanted to kick himself. "For Brandon."

Ross gave his arm a pat. "I thought you might be taking up the sport." He chuckled.

"I can arrange a slab with our concrete guys if you're really interested."

Kelsey sent Ross a frown. "Don't you think you should check that with Ava, Quinn?" She turned to him. "She's been protective—"

"She's changing." He'd jumped to her defense too quickly.

Ross's brows lifted while Kelsey's face brightened. "We noticed."

Her innuendo hadn't been lost on Quinn. He fought the heat that rose up his collar.

Kelsey craned her neck. "Ava's not here today?" She turned to Quinn. "Anything wrong?"

Quinn tried to be lighthearted. "I was going to ask you, but you're right about the hoop. I'll give Ava a call."

Kelsey rose and rested her hand on his shoulder. "Good idea. A riled mother is dangerous."

They all laughed, but with Ava's swinging moods, Kelsey was right. He didn't want to take even the smallest chance riling her. Another thing he didn't want was her friend's speculation about their relationship. He wished he knew what it was. Friendship had passed as far as he was concerned. Ava's presence brightened his life. She and Brandon filled his mind. Yet he sat with her friends unable to admit to himself, let alone to them, he was falling in love.

If he cared that much, he needed to take bigger steps forward.

Quinn stood and took the last swig of his coffee. As he headed toward the door and unable to resist, he grabbed a doughnut and napkin. He'd eat it in the car while he called Ava.

Ava hung up the phone and looked at Brandon. "That was Quinn. He was worried about you."

"Me?" His brows raised, but she noted a faint pleased look sneaking to his face. "I suppose he thought we missed church because I was sick."

"He did."

"Did you tell him the truth, Mom?"

She chuckled. "Yes, and don't blame me. We could have both set our alarms. That way when one of us forgets we'll have a backup."

Brandon rose from the table, stretched his back and picked up his breakfast dishes. "I'm feeling a lot better. I guess bed rest was the answer."

"That and getting the fear off your mind." She captured

his gaze. "You can't fool me, Bran. We were both worried it could be the Hodgkin's again."

He didn't try to cover the truth this time. "Okay, you're right." He set his bowl and cup in the sink and spun around. "So is Quinn coming over?"

"No."

Disappointment shrouded his face before he turned away. She grinned to herself. "We're going over there."

He spun back. "We? Does that mean I can get back to work?"

"You can do a little if Quinn agrees. He's protective of you."

A harrumph shot from Brandon's throat. "Not as protective as—" He turned to her. "Okay, you're doing better, but you were the protection champ, Mom."

Ava chuckled, loving the new relationship they'd developed since she'd made an effort to back off. She had to thank Quinn for that.

After sending Brandon to get ready, she slipped into a pair of denim capris and a striped polo shirt. After slipping her feet into her sandals, she grabbed her handbag and met Bran waiting by the dining room doorway to the side porch.

During the short car ride, her thoughts slipped back to the last time she'd seen Quinn. The kiss. Her wavering emotions. It all confused her. And then she still clung to her concern.

Since seeing Dreams Come True pop up in the letter from his attorney, she'd spent time weighing what it meant. Quinn never talked about his business. She knew it involved software but what about it? Sometimes with his closed-up manner, she wondered if he were having business problems. And why was Dreams Come True in the letter? If Quinn were wealthy, he might be the foundation's anonymous donor. That mystery would be solved, but that wasn't likely. Instead, she suspected it involved a special trip for Brandon, but if that were so, he should have talked with her first. She still didn't want to travel too far away from his oncologist or the hospital. Still, the possibility hung in her mind. Quinn had come into their lives and sometimes she sensed she'd lost control of her life. Yes, Brandon needed a man's influence, but sometimes he'd taken over and not only Brandon, but her.

When they arrived, Quinn was working in the front yard, trimming the shrubbery beneath the oversize French pane windows. The house became more beautiful each time she visited.

Quinn gave a wave from the front walk, and Brandon darted from the car, bounding to him as he did with his buddies. Quinn had taken to Bran like a child to a puppy. He slipped his arm around Brandon's shoulder, and they headed up the porch steps, leaving her striding up the sidewalk alone.

Once again, she'd become the outsider, and she didn't like the feeling. She had to take some of the blame. She realized now that hidden inside her was a longing to feel complete, the need for someone to love her, too. But had she let that inner need blind her from what was best for her son. Maybe Quinn's strong character was too much for her. She needed someone, but a man who allowed her to be in charge of her son. In charge. In control. The words drained her spirit. She'd wanted to step back, loosen the reins, let Brandon become an adult. Her mind bogged with confusion.

Before digging too deep into her problem, Quinn returned to the porch and down the steps. "I'm glad you came."

Looking into his eyes brought her back from the doldrums. At this moment, she saw a friend, a man who cared about her and her son.

Quinn slipped his arm around her shoulders, then let it drop. "Brandon's here. I'd better be careful."

She agreed, not wanting to lose the progress they'd made with him. "Where is he?"

"I asked him to pour lemonade for all of us." He brushed her hand with his as they walked side by side. "I want him to feel welcome and comfortable here, and I do care. You know that."

"I know you do."

He paused. "Before we go in, I want to ask you something important. I hope you'll say yes."

Her pulse skipped, anticipating his question. Though her dark thoughts had stepped back, she still heard an echoing voice. Be careful. Yet as she searched his face, their kiss filled her mind. "What is it?" She held her breath.

"I'd like to have a slab of concrete poured behind the garage and put up a basketball hoop."

Her expectation crumbled, replaced by an unexpected laugh. "You're doing this for Brandon?"

Quinn gave her a strange look and frowned. "Why did you laugh?"

She managed to camouflage her bemusement. "I don't know. You surprised me." From his expression, she realized Quinn had no idea what had triggered in her mind with the reference to asking her something important.

"Are you angry?" His eyes searched hers.

"No. I'm glad you asked." She pressed her lips together as she considered her response. "I still worry about him, but I know he shoots baskets at his friend's house when I'm not there surveilling him. So…" She formed the words that were so hard to say. "So I suppose it's all right if you'd want to go to that expense." Though she agreed for Brandon, her concern rose. The relationship had become a snowball picking up speed and growing out of control.

He rested his hand on her arm and gave it a squeeze. "Thanks. He'll enjoy coming here more, and—"

"What are you doing?"

Brandon's voice startled her. His gaze swept past her to Quinn and back. She was riddled with guilt.

Quinn gave her a glance, then retreated to Brandon. "I was proposing an idea to your mom."

His eyes narrowed as he studied Quinn's face. "What kind of idea?"

"About putting up a basketball hoop once I get a slab of concrete behind the garage."

Bran's suspicious expression broke to a smile. "Really?"

"Really." Quinn gave him a high five, and they headed into the kitchen.

Ava stood back, pondering the situation. With Quinn in the picture, her role as mother seemed trivial. Quinn took the glory while she carried the burden. The negative thoughts returned. Envy of Brandon's feelings for Quinn? Fear of losing control? Concern about Quinn's secrets? She struggled to make sense. Quinn was a good man. Every sign led to that. He'd done nothing to hurt them and everything to make life better. Bran needed a good man in his life. How could she belittle the relationship?

She followed them into the kitchen, grasped her lemonade and listened to Quinn give Brandon a list of what he wanted him to do outside. "Now if you start feeling tired, admit it, okay?"

"I will." He gave Quinn a guilty smile and veered into the family room and out the patio door.

Quinn released a sigh. "I hope things stay cool between Brandon and me. It'll be easier for both of us."

What did he mean by easier for both of us? She placed her drink on the table and waited.

Quinn sidled up to her. "So what's on your mind?"

Her heart lurched. "Decorating?"

"That's all?"

She squirmed, knowing he wanted a better response from her, but she'd never been more befuddled. Her emotions boiled in a cauldron of confusion. She grasped the first thought that struck her. "I found some things upstairs I'd like to show you."

Noting his expression, he verged on protesting, but she

didn't give in. She beckoned to him and strode through the family room to the staircase. Quinn's footsteps sounded behind her.

At the top of the stairs, she moved past the overlook into the family room—she steered him into the room where she'd found so many precious items. She peered out the window and spotted Brandon on his knees, digging small holes every few inches and tucking in the flowers.

When she turned back, Quinn stood so close she gave a gasp.

His arms slipped up her back and drew her close. "Brandon's in the garden, and we're up here. Alone."

His smile sent a warm rush through her, and in his arms, her fears scattered. He touched his lips to hers as he'd done before, but this time the touch revealed an amazing familiarity as if they'd kissed for a lifetime. They fit together, her arms around his back and his holding her close. The rhythm of his heart, his breathing, matched hers, and replacing her gasp, she uttered a sigh that joined his.

When he tilted back his head and looked into her eyes, her knees became melted ice cream, soft but sweet. "I never expected these feelings to happen, Ava. I thought my life had ended, but you've giving it back to me."

Images exploded in her mind like fireworks—what life had been and what it had become. "And we have a fender-bender to thank."

"A fender-denter." He grinned and gave her a hug before lowering his arms. "I suppose we'd better focus on business. What amazing things did you find?"

She'd forgotten. She opened one of the cartons and lifted out an amazing vase with a woven basket design in white adorned with tiny shamrocks. "This is Belleek, isn't it?"

"My Irish heritage. We purchased a few mementos in Ireland while visiting my family."

Her pulse skipped. "You have family in Ireland?"

"Aunts, uncles, cousins. Have you ever been there?"

Visions of photographs she'd seen filled her mind. "Never."

"Maybe you will one day."

Her lungs compressed with the thought. "I'd love that." More than love. She didn't have words to describe it. Pulling herself away from dreams, she dug into the carton and pulled out other Belleek items. "I want to use these downstairs. Any ideas?"

"You're the decorator."

She gave him a playful swat and placed the lovely pieces back in the carton. "Would you carry this down?"

He hoisted the box, and though she had more to investigate, she had something else important to accomplish. She followed him down the stairs and waited for him to set the box on the living room sofa, before heading for the family room door. When he stepped outside, she went to the kitchen and picked up her lemonade and joined him.

Quinn spoke with Brandon before retreating to the shaded patio.

After placing her drink on the umbrella table, Ava slipped into a chair and watched Brandon as she tried to initiate the burning issue. "It's wonderful seeing Brandon acting like himself."

"It is. His weakness alarmed me that day in the garden. Different from the day we met."

The image swept through her mind. "His remission has been over two years now. When you mentioned visiting Ireland, I recalled we haven't traveled anywhere since he was diagnosed."

"No?"

Ava explained her reason while she faced how fear had controlled her life and Bran's, too. "That needs to change."

"Another step in the right direction. Letting go." He gave her a lingering look.

The conversation had moved in the right direction, and she drew on her courage. "Have you ever heard of Dreams Come True Foundation?"

Quinn jerked when she said the name. "Yes, why?"

"They offer trips and things for kids who've been sick. I never took advantage of the opportunity because of Bran's illness. I could never afford some of the things they do for the children." She followed his every move, detecting a look of discomfort washing over his face.

"Contact them. Why not? More than two years in remission is a positive achievement."

Confusion reigned in her head. She'd expected him to discourage her or admit he'd been planning an event for Brandon. Still he'd asked her permission about the basketball hoop. He certainly would have asked her about Dreams Come True.

She lifted her lemonade and took a sip, feeling her cheeks tighten as much as her chest had done with all her rambling.

Quinn rose and headed back to Brandon while she sat in silence, dealing with the questions rampaging her mind.

Chapter Ten

Quinn stood with his shoulder against the bedroom door-frame and watched Ava amble around the room, her index finger pressed against her lips, pausing for a moment in thought before moving to another area. Each time he gazed at her lips his mind glided back to the upstairs room and the kiss they'd shared.

A week had passed since they'd been together. He'd concentrated on the concrete slab he'd had laid behind the garage, and he'd purchased a basketball hoop and hired someone to hang it. Though he was anxious for Brandon to see it, he hadn't yet. He'd been tied up with school activities—studying for exams with his buddies and finishing his last projects while still recuperating from mono. Though his color had improved, his energy hadn't returned. Brandon's situation continued to plague him.

He was eager to show Brandon the hoop, but a greater anxiety overshadowed this. Ava had been quiet all day, so unlike her, and he'd wondered if it had anything to do with her question about Dreams Come True.

The next day he'd noticed a letter from his lawyer in the stack on the desk where Ava had spilled the water. It had been deep in the stack and never entered his mind that she might have seen it. If she had, he worried she suspected something, but he didn't know what her mind would concoct. Or did she suspect the truth—he was the foundation's donor? He'd heard numerous times from his attorney that being anonymous raised people's curiosity. The decision had been his, and his reason made sense to him.

His attention shifted to Ava, standing in a corner of the room, looking lost. "Ava, what's wrong?"

Her head snapped in his direction, a dazed look on her face.

He grinned. "You called me in here, but I don't know why."

She came to life and released a sigh. "I'm stymied."

"About what?"

She pulled something glossy from her pocket and opened it. "I was planning to go for this."

She handed him a torn page from a magazine, a room decorated with tropical influences—bamboo, palm leaf prints, a jar of seashells. He eyed her, deciding if he should be honest or tell her he liked it. "It's tropical."

"That's what I planned, but I found the beautiful pieces from Ireland, and now I'm thinking an Irish look might be better. The green-toned walls work for either motif."

His chest filled with recollections of his walks along the sea, the rugged causeway and stretches of green—every shade imaginable with rolling hills and stone cottages. He wanted to make her happy but he decided to be honest. "Ireland means the most to me."

A smile broke from her musing as her eyes captured his. "I love it."

He moved closer to her, slipped his arm behind her back and gave her a hug. His lips ached to greet hers, but she'd been reserved since she'd arrived so he forced his arm lower and drifted back to the door. "That's settled. Let's take a break. I want to talk to you about something anyway."

A questioning look sprang to her face. He didn't address it. Instead he strode to the family room with her behind him.

Ava passed the sofa, her usual spot, and stepped to the patio window. "Let's sit outside. The garden's beautiful." She grasped the doorknob, the sun throwing colorful prisms through the beveled glass design, and opened the door.

A warm breeze floated through the screen, and he filled his lungs with fresh air as he stepped onto the patio and joined her on the glider. "Are you okay?" He ached to cuddle her in his arms. Instead he cupped her hand in his.

She tilted her head, a look of contentment on her face he hadn't recognized earlier.

Deciding how to approach the subject muddied his mind. The silence lengthened while he knew he had to say something. "Are you happy with your job here?"

"You know I love it." She studied him a moment before giving his arm a pat. "But that's not what you want to talk about, is it?"

"No." He decided to barrel ahead. "When Brandon was struggling with his decision to make an oncologist appointment, I wanted to encourage him."

She cocked her head, her eyes questioning.

"I told him when he was feeling better I'd support him about getting his learner's permit."

A look spread over her face that he didn't expect and didn't like.

"I—I know you have Bran's well-being at heart, but—" She bit her upper lip, her face reflecting an ensuing struggle. "But sometimes I resent your influence on Brandon." She evaded his eyes. "I know that sounds awful. I'm thrilled that Brandon finally has a male that can see through his eyes. You understand things I never will about a teenage boy, but I'm his mother. I'm trying to give him freedom, and yet…" Her jaw tensed as she turned away.

He slipped his arm around her and drew her closer, but

despite his attempt to apologize, his lungs depleted. "Ava, please. Maybe I have overstepped my bounds with Brandon. I sensed that you appreciated my—"

"I do, Quinn. I really do."

A tear dripped from her cheek and struck his hand. He brushed the moisture from her cheeks, wrestling with his own emotions. "I need to tell you something."

Her inquisitive gaze inched to his.

A deep ache rose from his chest and settled in his throat as he sought words he'd never spoken to anyone. "I wasn't the best father to my son, Ava."

A stunned expression darkened her face. "That's not true."

"It's too true. Trust me."

Her doubting eyes captured his. "You're wonderful with Brandon. You're kind and have more patience than I've ever had."

"And I should have had that kind of patience with my son." A knot tangled in his throat. "Since that horrible day, God's helped me through the pain. I grieved for what I hadn't done. I hated myself for not being a better father. I—"

"Quinn, I don't understand." Her head shook like leaves in a storm. "No. You're—"

He rested his hand on her arm. "Believe me. My business had taken over my life. It had become a success, far greater than I had anticipated. I became money hungry. Success hungry. Power hungry. It became my all in all."

As if she understood, a tender look filled her eyes. "Family should be your all in all."

"God should have been my all in all. If He had, my values would have been different and my family would have received my love and attention. Instead my company took precedence." Hearing the words tore at his sinew. He swallowed the bitter memories. "I've changed. Now the Lord is my all in all. That's made the difference."

Her eyes filled with a depth of understanding he struggled

to comprehend. Her arms slipped around his back, and for the first time, she drew him against her. "I don't know what to say. I'm heartbroken to hear what you've been through, but I admire who you are now, and that's all that counts."

He longed to tell her everything but still was not ready. He'd asked her to trust him, but he struggled with the ability to trust her with the truth. Quinn prayed one day he could confess all the things in his heart.

Ava had spent days wrestling her thoughts. When she heard Quinn's story, her concerns eased. He had the need to be a better father, and he made up for his mistake with Brandon. But Bran wasn't his son, and would Quinn slide back into his old habit if he were? Those things happened. Asking moot questions served no purpose. Time would tell. She needed to trust her gut as well as her head. She pushed the struggle from her mind, trying to accept the good influence Quinn had on Brandon without feeling envious. And she couldn't lie to herself. Quinn made her feel desirable and complete.

She eyed her shrimp-toned arms and moved her chair into the shade. Mesmerized by Bran and Quinn shooting hoops, she'd lost judgment on time in the sun. She knew better. Though born with brown hair and eyes, her skin remained fair. She and the sun's battle began in late spring.

Since Tom had died, Memorial Day passed by like any other day, but Quinn deemed the day worthy of a celebration. Though the picnic took place in his backyard, she could think of no better location for the event. He loved the garden flowers blooming around her, the shrubs well-trimmed and the birds diving into the birdbath. And she'd had a part in it.

Her heart lurched picturing Bran's face when he stepped onto the patio and spotted the basketball hoop. Quinn had proposed the idea to him, but Bran's expression let her know he didn't expect it to happen. He'd been disappointed many times by his dad. Thinking about their money situation rendered her distraught. She'd never wanted Brandon to know about his dad's horrible investment mistake.

Her pulse skidded when she saw Brandon run backward, ward off Quinn's flailing arms and make a basket. Though proud, her natural instinct triggered concern for his health. If she could let it go and trust his remission as a blessing, her mind would ease, but her worry remained. She needed to pray harder. Trust. The word turned her stomach. She failed miserably.

"Did you see that, Mom?"

She managed to grin and applauded.

Quinn gave her a wink. "Are you bored? You could join us."

"Me? Never."

"Come on, Mom. Give it a try." Brandon beckoned to her.

Clinging to the chair, she shook her head, but their persistence didn't stop. She gave up and rose, knowing she and basketball was a bad idea.

The two men tossed the ball back and forth as if she wasn't there. As she watched, she calculated the timing, and at the right moment, she leaped forward and captured the ball. She knew enough to bounce it as she stepped away, and when she had a chance, she veered around Quinn and flipped the ball into the air. To her shock, it fell through the hoop.

"Mom." Brandon's wide eyes filled with pride as he captured the ball. "I didn't know you could play."

"Neither did I." She pressed her hand against her chest, as astounded as he was.

Quinn gave her a high five, and she made a quick decision. "I'm retiring on a high note."

"Come on. You can't do that." He grasped her arm and pulled her close while her discomfort overtook her.

She eyed her watch. "Shouldn't we be thinking about

food?" She motioned toward the grill. "I'll go inside and make the salad if you'll heat the grill."

He checked the hour and nodded. "It is about that time." He rested his hand on Brandon's shoulder. "We need a rest anyway."

Though Brandon nodded, she knew her son well enough to see he didn't want to stop.

He wiped perspiration from his forehead with the bottom of his T-shirt and approached Quinn. "What can I do?"

"Do you know how to start the grill?"

Bran grinned. "Who doesn't?"

"Okay. You can get that going, and I'll go inside and get the burgers ready."

Having a job seemed to reconcile him, and Brandon marched to the grill. He turned on the gas as she stepped onto the patio and headed inside.

In moments, Quinn arrived, stopping to wash his hands in the sink before opening the refrigerator. She stood beside him pulling out the makings for a salad, enjoying the coolness of the fridge but more conscious of the warmth she felt beside Quinn.

With her hands full, Quinn took advantage of the situation and drew her into his arms while she balanced the head of lettuce, a cucumber and two tomatoes. "Not fair." She wiggled in his arms.

But he only chuckled, holding her close. "All is fair in love and war." He lowered his head, his lips joining hers.

Though she delighted in his touch, she feared Brandon would come through the door and witness Quinn's affection.

Quinn read her mind and shifted back. "I know." He tilted his head toward the patio. "But I can't resist."

She ducked past him, shaking the only free index finger she could spare.

His grin changed when she heard the patio door open and

close, and Brandon stepped into the kitchen. "Grills getting ready." His gaze shifted from her to Quinn. "Did I interrupt?"

Ava's heart skipped a beat. "Not one bit." She set the vegetables beside the sink, taking time to gain her composure. If Brandon suspected a romance brewing, she had no idea what would happen.

He settled onto a kitchen chair. "I hoped I had."

The comment threw her. "Interrupted?"

He nodded, a quirky grin on his face.

Her breathing shallowed. "What were you expecting?" Her mind froze as she waited for his answer.

"I hoped you agreed for me to get my learner's permit."

She knew Quinn's promise, but the comment raked her anyway. "No, I haven't."

Quinn's gaze shot to Brandon, his discomfort evident. "No progress yet. Sorry, Bran."

It was the first time she'd heard Quinn call him by his nickname. A feeling of futility washed over her. She knew it was coming, but they'd talked and she'd told him how she felt.

She kept her back to them rinsing the tomatoes. "Don't you think it's my decision, Brandon?" She turned, managing to control the irritation in her voice.

Quinn broke his silence. "It wasn't like that, Ava. I know how you feel, but a promise is a promise."

The comment caught her. "I don't see the rush. You can't drive until you're seventeen. You have more than a year to wait to get your driver's license."

"That's not true." Quinn came to his rescue again. "A learner's permit allows him to drive with you or another adult. He'll get practice."

Her back stiffened. Two against one again.

"Yeah, Mom, once I get my Segment 2 driver's permit and I'm sixteen, I can drive during the day by myself."

She felt trapped. "I have reasons for hesitating, you know. This isn't a whim. I'm not trying to be a bad mother."

Brandon's expression had sunk from his grin to desperation. "Mom, you act like we're plotting against you. Quinn only said if I saw the oncologist and got better, he'd be on my side for the permit."

"I know he did."

"Ava, I—" Quinn's mouth closed, and he lowered his eyes. "I'm sorry. I explained my reason to you."

"I know." Seeing the two men shrivel in front of her didn't halt her irritation. Maybe she'd said things she shouldn't, but she had rights. Yet again she'd turned her gratefulness into bitter ingratitude. But today wasn't the day for an argument. This was between her and Quinn. She held up her hand. "Let's drop this. Please." She eyed them both. "I'm sorry I ruined the afternoon."

"You didn't ruin—"

"Let's drop it." She fought to keep her tears at bay. Her emotions swayed from pleasure to bitterness. She no longer made sense, and the battle of head and heart made her weary. Quinn had emotionally adopted Brandon to replace his son. "My main problem with rushing to get the license is we have one car. The sooner Brandon can drive the more he'll want to use my car, and I'm not comfortable being stranded without one, or he'll want a car, and I...I can't afford a car along with all the extra insurance." She resented the admission.

Brandon stood, his expression thoughtful. "Mom, I know about the problem. I'll get a job and save for a car. I just want to get my driver's license like my friends. Some days when you're tired, maybe I could run to the store for you or—"

She held up her palm. "Brandon, I'm giving up. You can have your learner's permit. You've been through enough. I know it's important to you. We'll work things out." She waved her hand as if she could make the situation go away. "Now, let's enjoy our picnic."

Though the tension hung in the silence, she turned back to the salad. Bran washed his hands and helped Quinn form the burgers. As time passed, Quinn and Brandon's conversation eased the tension, but her mental struggle remained. If Quinn would ever have a part in their lives, she had to make the decision to accept Quinn's part in her son's life or end their relationship. Another head and heart issue she wasn't sure she could conquer.

Chapter Eleven

Quinn stared through the window into the backyard, trying to decide what he wanted to do. Since Memorial Day, Ava had been cordial on the phone but made excuses why she couldn't see him. He'd even agreed to go shopping for the items she wanted for the house. She'd still put him off.

He relived their picnic when he tried to keep the afternoon going with Brandon and draw Ava into the conversation. She'd talked a little, but he felt the strain, and after Ava and Brandon left, he reviewed all that had happened and didn't know how to resolve the problem without stepping out of the relationship, and he couldn't do that.

Maybe he'd gone overboard with the boy. He'd muddled his relationship with Sean, and he wanted to do it right with Brandon. Though Brandon wasn't his son, he cared about him more than he could say. And Ava. He didn't have words to express his feelings, but he had little control over their relationship. One minute their friendship seemed to blossom even deeper, and the next, she attacked him for getting involved in her life.

His brother's cautious take on Ava and his wealth hadn't influenced him. She knew he owned a business, but she didn't know how much he was worth. Though she'd accepted the check for her and Brandon's work and the car repair, with other monetary help, she'd backed away. If she were money-grubbing, she would have taken everything he offered.

And she was honest. He'd left her in the house alone for two days, and she respected his possessions and had worked diligently while he was gone. The letter concerned him. She'd made one reference to the Dreams Come True Foundation and nothing more, so he could have been wrong about her suspicion. And what if he told her? The idea rattled in his head. He could only do that when he felt confident in their relationship. Right now, she confused him so often.

His brother popped into his mind again. Curious as to what his brother would think of Ava, he pulled out his cell phone and hit his number, but all he reached was Liam's voice mail. "Give me a call when you have a minute." Frustrated, he hung up, ambled into the family room and plopped on the sofa.

The situation with Brandon remained in turmoil. He'd thought about offering to buy Brandon a car, but now he couldn't decide how Ava would react to that. A new car cost thousands, and he knew her well enough to anticipate her response.

But a used car could be different. He could buy one from someone he trusted. He recalled people he knew and businesses he respected. Randy at the collision shop came to mind. He might suggest a possibility or know someone who could.

He settled back, punched in the numbers and waited. Randy's sister answered and called him to the phone. The conversation took only a moment with the promise he'd look around and give him a call if he found a lead.

After hanging up, Quinn's senses returned. Searching for a used car was a waste of time if Ava said no, and right now the car would be a touchy subject. Determined to resolve the issues between them, he pulled the car keys from his pocket and strode into the garage. She could dismiss him on the telephone, but doing it face-to-face might be more difficult. He was willing to take the chance.

The ten-minute trip offered time to formulate a plan, but the plan failed at every turn. When he spotted her street, he hesitated. Turning around made more sense than making an already complex problem worse. But his heart won the struggle. He put his wisdom on hold and turned left onto Blair Street.

Ava's car sat in the driveway, and when he spotted it, his pulse accelerated. Would she slam the door in his face or invite him in? He pulled behind her car, pausing a moment to send up a prayer. God knew his intentions were good. He prayed Ava recognized the spirit of his visit.

As he headed up the front walk, Brandon's curtain shifted, and he waved. Before he reached the door, the boy opened it, a smile lighting his face. "Come in. Mom didn't tell me you called."

He wet his lips. "I didn't call." He rallied his confidence. "I hope she'll—" He faltered, seeing Ava eyeing him from the dining room.

"Quinn." She strode toward him. "What are you doing here?"

The question hung in the air until he sorted out the truth. "I wanted to see you."

She gave him a questioning look.

"To talk."

She seemed to weigh his response. "Come in." She stepped back and watched him take a seat in one of the easy chairs.

Brandon plopped on the sofa, his grin still evident.

If he had his wishes, Quinn preferred Brandon to leave the room. Trying to discuss their problems with him nearby only added to the stress. His mind was a jumble until he set his plan in action. "You'd ask me about shopping for the items you still need, and I wondered when you wanted to do that."

Though he saw a spark ignite in her eyes, she tried to cover her interest. "The end of school is a busy time for me. I'm tired at the end of the day."

"Sorry. I forgot it's the end of the school year." He counted the seconds before she gave a nod, but he sensed her desire to shop was overpowering her frustration with him.

Brandon squirmed in the chair, his attention shifting from him to his mother and back as if he were waiting for some profound discussion that involved him, but Quinn was smarter than that. He wanted the boy to be bored, and he knew he was winning.

"I'll let you guys talk about shopping." He gave a disappointed shrug and sauntered from the room.

Relief swished through Quinn as he watched the teen vanish into the hallway. When Brandon's bedroom door gave a click, he caved against the chair back, his eyes clinging to Ava's.

She looked away and slipped onto the sofa. "Is that why you came?"

Her inflection confused him. Was she questioning his motive or dismissing him? A response caught in his throat until an honest one found its way out. "What's wrong with us, Ava?"

"Us?"

The question shouldn't have confused her. He didn't respond.

"You mean what's wrong with me."

"I mean us. We've had great times together. You've enjoyed decorating the house and I've loved what you've done. We've had some honest talks." The feel of her lips on his wavered through his mind. "And some special moments. We've grown, but—" Words escaped him.

"But I knot up, and you don't get it." Her gaze shifted to the carpet.

"I don't." He questioned his response. "You've thanked me for my friendship to Brandon." He realized the volume of his voice and lowered it. "I care about him, Ava. I'm not placating you or trying to pretend he's my son." His heart squeezed. "He's not. Sean is dead. Nothing will bring him back, not even another fifteen-year-old boy."

Ava's face darkened as she faced him. "I know that. I'm just… I don't know what I am. A mother who's losing control over her son." The reality darkened her face, and she closed her eyes. "Do you realize the effort I put into Brandon's health after he was diagnosed? He became my life. My focus. Everything led to him. And now—"

"Ava."

A distraught expression dimmed her face.

"Now you feel extraneous. You feel you've lost your purpose." Her expression ripped at his heart.

"Bran said something a while ago that I keep remembering. He said I don't have a life. I'm living his." She winced as the words tumbled out. "It's true. I forgot how to live, and when I lose control of his life, I don't know what to do."

"Live your own, Ava." He rose and sank to the cushion beside her. "You have so much to give, and not only to Brandon, but to…to me."

Her eyes searched his. "Quinn, we help each other in many ways. I didn't realize how lonely I was until you came into the picture. My days dragged by, marked by my job, my house, my finances and my worry about Brandon. That's it."

He recognized his own life reflected in hers except he tacked on his continuing guilt. "But it's different now, isn't it?"

She nodded. "But I fight it, don't I?"

He slipped his arm around her back. "Ava, I want to do things for you and Brandon. I came here today to offer to buy a car for Brandon so that you wouldn't have to worry about having only one car. I want to make life easier, and—"

"A car?" She closed her eyes. "Why, because you pity me? You have money, and I don't?"

The question dug deep. "No, because I care about both of you." But that wasn't the whole truth, and the time had come to let it go. "I suppose I'm trying to live better than I did. I told you I wasn't the best father, but I didn't tell you the whole story."

Concern sparked in her eyes.

The memory tore through his mind. "It's what happened the day Sean and Lydia died."

The words were out, and as he let the story find its way from the recesses of his core, a calm settled over him. The insurance payment and his hatred for it lost its power. He'd harbored the pain so long it had become the proverbial mole-hill that turned into a mountain.

The tension in Ava's body gave way, and she sank against him, her arm slipping around his back, a look so deep in her eyes he felt she saw his soul.

She raised her hand and cupped his cheek. "Did you ever think that if you had been driving it may have made no difference at all? You and Sean may have died in the accident instead?"

Ice ran through his veins. "No. Impossible. I was the better driver. It was my—"

"You're not invincible, Quinn. You make mistakes. With Sean at the wheel, any driver was at a disadvantage. Trying to steer away from the crash from the passenger seat would have been nearly impossible. Can't you see that?"

"But Lydia had fewer hours behind the wheel, and…" His words faded. His reasoning failed. Ava's comment nailed him to the seat.

She touched his hand. "If you and Sean had died, Lydia would have been left alone now dealing with rebuilding her life and struggling with a business that she couldn't run."

The reality pressed the air from his lungs. "Lydia ran our home. She knew nothing about the business." She would have been lost.

Ava looked at him, her eyes filled with a tenderness he'd

never experienced. "In my Bible studies…" She gave a tilt of her head. "I've been away from the Word so long I started reading it again. I started with Ecclesiastes, and now I'm reading Jeremiah. This morning I read verses that touched me, but now, I'm thinking they were there to equip me."

She'd lost him. "Equip you for what?"

She raised her index finger. "Wait a minute and I'll get my Bible."

Dazed at the direction of the conversation, he watched her vanish through the doorway to the hall. Alone, his ears picked up the *thump-thump* of rock music reverberating from Brandon's room. In the intensity of their conversation, he hadn't noticed.

Ava returned with the Bible and began her search. She flipped through pages, turned back and then forward again. She paused, her eyes focused on a page.

He tried to imagine what she wanted to share with him. Jeremiah focused on God's ultimate judgment and the importance of repentance. Did Ava think that's what he needed?

"Here it is." She handed him the Bible. "Start at Jeremiah 29:11 and go down to here." She pointed to a verse below.

He scanned the scripture, his chest constricting with the image forming on his brain. Without need for contemplation, the verses spoke volumes. He understood what he'd been and where he'd come, and he understood the reason for what happened.

"Read it out loud." Ava gave him a nudge.

Refusal would only emphasize his flaw. *"'For I know the plans I have for you,' declares the Lord, 'plans to prosper you and not to harm you, plans to give you hope and a future. Then you will call upon me and come and pray to me, and I will listen to you. You will seek me and find me when you seek me with all your heart. I will be found by you,' declares the Lord, 'and will bring you back from captivity.'"* His heart weighted with the truth. "The Lord equipped you with this verse for me. Is that what you meant?"

She offered a guilty nod. "For both of us."

Ava had recognized his need, but the reality that had to be drilled into him was losing his life to gain riches. And losing eternal life with his focus on wealth and success. But after the disaster, he'd sought the Lord with all his heart and he'd atoned. Now he'd used his money for others.

"Please don't think I'm criticizing you." Ava's hand squeezed his. "I understand now why you want to give so much, but I don't understand why you hide it. You don't live like a man with money. Is your business in trouble? Why don't you talk about it? You're so secretive."

Brandon's music pounded in his ears along with the beat of his heart. "My business, the insurance money and the lawsuit." Her questions reverberated in his mind. *Is your business in trouble?* His mind snapped. "Ava, what do you mean I'm so secretive?"

"I know you own a business, but does it provide enough money to waste on us?" She held up her hand to stop his comment. "And please don't misunderstand. You have a nice house, but it's not a mansion. You drive an SUV not a Mercedes. It's like you're living a double life."

He couldn't believe what he'd heard. She thought… He clasped his hands together rather than slap them over his ears. Getting a grip, Quinn swallowed. "Ava, I don't spend money I don't have. I don't talk about business with you because it's boring, and I told you I am trying to change the way I live my life. I don't want to focus on the treasures on earth."

"You're not involved in any pyramid schemes or…?"

"I can't believe what you're asking me." He lowered his head, still disbelieving her insinuation. "I have a lucrative business. A large corporation. I would never be involved in anything illegal." Stunned, he stared at her trying to make sense out of her implication.

She gazed at him, contrition written in her eyes. "I'm sorry. I don't know what's—"

"Ava, I care enough about you to end your delusion."

Her face paled.

Though he'd lashed out, he halted his apology. She needed to hear the truth, no matter what happened to their relationship. "I left a voice mail for my brother this morning. He'd said he'd like to come for a visit and see what you've done to the house. I know you want to finish the bedroom first, but I'd like you to meet Liam and Jen. Maybe then you'll see me in a different light. Maybe you'll understand."

"Please, Quinn. I shouldn't have said what I did."

"It's too late. You said it. My honesty is important to me. You're not making sense but I want you to know the truth."

"Quinn, I have a serious trust issue, and I need to tell you about my hus—"

"When's dinner?"

Brandon's voice split the air. The vibration of the music had stopped, and Quinn had missed the sound of the teen's door opening and his footsteps. All he heard was Ava's continued distrust in him. He should walk away, but he couldn't. He'd learned forgiveness from the Bible, and he followed it— except for his own failures. And he couldn't back away with his heart tangled in their lives.

Ava's eyes, shifted from Brandon to her watch, and her stunned expression faded. "We'll eat soon."

With their conversation going nowhere, Quinn rose. "I'll let you get to dinner."

"Wednesday. I can drop by after work for shopping." Her face tensed with what looked like regret.

Quinn agreed and strode to the front door before anymore was said. So many things had been left hanging, but now he needed to think, and so did she.

Ava placed the last package in Quinn's bedroom. Though they'd shopped, their time together had been a bust. They'd focused on their purchases. She found numerous items for the Irish decor—a gorgeous rug featuring a design from the eighth century Book of Kells, a Celtic throw and a lovely framed print of the traditional Irish Blessings, May The Road Rise Up. Her greatest find was the map of Ireland in shades of green and beige framed in a walnut frame. The wood complemented Quinn's bedroom set. Every purchase complemented the shades of green in the bedroom—a darker hue on the fireplace wall, a lighter shades throughout and the woodwork painted in a cream color.

Her admission about Tom and her unwarranted concern about Quinn still hadn't been addressed. Brandon had ended that discussion, and Quinn didn't bring up the topics on their shopping spree, and she didn't, either, since it wasn't a good time to talk.

The sound of the telephone collided with the quiet. She sank into the easy chair and closed her eyes. The room relaxed her, and she needed the sense of comfort. Their complicated relationship left her dangling. Her emotions felt raw.

She pushed her weight from the chair and strode through the bedroom door. As she passed Quinn's office, she caught a movement. She watched him spin around and stop her. "Let's talk a minute."

His abrupt request caught her off guard, but she entered the room and sat in the only other chair available.

"I just heard from Randy at B & B Collision. I'd called him on leads to a used car. I knew you'd reject the idea of a new car for Brandon so I figured I'd have a better chance with an older one."

Once again, Quinn had taken over her responsibility. She held her breath, waiting for the rest of the car issue.

Quinn eyed her. "I trust Randy, and I hoped he might know of someone ready to sell. He does. It's a four-year-old sedan, sports model. It's in good shape. Bright red. No rust.

Randy said the motor is good. What do you think? I have to let him know."

Quinn's eagerness pounded against her determination. "Bran doesn't have his permit yet, and I can't let you buy him a car."

"I gave that thought already. Bran said he'd get a job so I'll hire him, and he can work it off."

The look on his face let her know he had his ammunition ready to go. "Come on, Quinn. He's planted the flowers. You have everything painted inside, vinyl trim outside and a new roof. What more can he do?"

"Mow the lawn. Trim. Prune. Weed."

If he had ammo, so did she. "Let's see. We have ten weeks in the summer at about twenty dollars a week. Hmm? Are you telling me you can purchase this car for two hundred dollars?" She arched her brow, hoping she'd made a point.

"I'd pay Brandon more than twenty dollars a week. It's worth a hundred to me."

"That is too much, and you know it. Let me think about it, Quinn. Maybe I can come up with a way to pay you." She managed to stay calm. "These silly arguments are wearing us thin. Let's work at cooperation."

His expression faded as she squelched his scheme. Though her heart longed to accept all that he offered, along with his kisses, her head told her to be wise. But her sound mind seemed to crumble at every turn.

She weighed his expression, a grin growing on his face, and she saw his rebuttal heading her way. Even now he made her smile.

She blocked it with her palm. "Don't argue with me. I'm going home, but I'll be here Saturday to finish your bedroom."

"You want me to cooperate."

She suspected that would be a challenge.

She stepped into the hallway before she remembered. "Did you talk with your brother?"

"I did. You'll meet him a week from next Friday."

She peeked back into his office. "That's my birthday." She ducked out and hurried to the front door before he could say anything.

Chapter Twelve

Ava stood in Quinn's master suite and gazed at the lovely room. Quinn had spent the afternoon at church involved in a cleanup day while she'd done everything she planned to finish the room. She hoped he liked the way everything in the room fell together. She smoothed the deep green spread and eyed the Ireland map she'd hung at the head of the bed. The carpet and throw set off the fireplace as she'd pictured.

The surprise she'd accomplished on her own caused her concern, but she hoped that he'd healed enough to accept what she'd done. She gazed at the four photographs of Quinn, Lydia and Sean she'd found in their snapshots from Ireland. Though years younger, they reflected happier times with views of the green rolling hills and the crystal lakes below, sheep grazing in a green meadow, and three smiling faces looking out over three glorious lakes.

Pride pumped her spirit. She loved decorating and Quinn had given her the opportunity to use her talents. Her optimism sank when she pictured meeting his brother. What would he think of her talent, but even more importantly, what would he think of her?

Quinn said meeting her brother would help her know him better. She sank under the weight of her earlier accusation.

From all she'd witnessed, Quinn showed every good quality a woman would want in a man. His generosity and kindness went beyond anyone's expectations. He believed in the Lord and attended church. Air drained from her chest. She gripped the doorframe to steady herself, trying to make sense of her unwarranted fears.

Leaving her handiwork, she strode into the family room and paused at the wide window looking into the garden. Every day offered a new surprise, new flowers opening to the sun, new blossoms sprouting on shrubs and new birds drinking from the birdbath. As she watched a cedar waxwing dipped into the water and flew off again. Her heart soared with it.

New experiences. New sights. New awareness. Each day her life opened to newness. She'd experienced new thoughts and shopped in new stores, ones Quinn could afford and she couldn't. And she'd become aware of many new things. Loneliness left her empty, but Quinn's presence gave her life. Hopelessness left her frightened. God's love and promises gave her hope.

She forced herself from the window and made her way to the kitchen. Her light-headedness had eased, but her stomach rebelled. It wanted food. Quinn had even been generous with his kitchen. Searching inside the refrigerator, she located a loaf of bread and an apple. Chuckling at Quinn's empty fridge, she explored the pantry and found peanut butter and jelly. She loved it.

After making a sandwich, she stepped outside and bit into the bread, wishing she'd remembered to bring out a drink. Too lazy to go back inside, she took a bite of the apple, letting the moisture blend with the peanut butter. Life could be an adventure, too, discovering new ways to deal with problems.

Thoughts of Quinn prodded her line of thought—his business, his lifestyle, his generosity. Though they didn't match, she would be stupid not to realize Quinn had money. A few days ago he'd offered to purchase a car for Brandon. He'd wanted to hire a plumber for her. He'd paid her car repair bill. He'd taken her to an expensive restaurant. He'd purchased expensive items to add to the decor. Why did she question the success of his business? Then probably that's where his brother came in.

After her talk with Quinn, she'd realized he could be the secret donor to the Dreams Come True Foundation. He'd mentioned insurance money and the lawsuit. With his confessed guilty feeling about the money he received from them, she could imagine him refusing to use it for his good. Yet giving it to others in need made sense.

She pressed her hand to her chest. If Quinn were the donor, why hadn't he told her? She closed her eyes and massaged her temples where the pounding hurt the most. She already knew the answer. She was a talker, and she had lots of friends with an interest in Dreams Come True. Quinn didn't think she could keep his secret. She didn't understand why it had to be a secret, but giving anonymously seemed important to him.

Her mind wrestled with the possibility. If he didn't trust her, any hope of forging a relationship would turn to ash. Her earlier thoughts shamed her again. She'd doubted Quinn's honesty and even told him so, yet he hadn't shut her out. Her head spun.

She rose, carrying the plate and apple core, and reached for the doorknob. Before she turned it, the door opened. She gasped.

Quinn stepped back. "Sorry. I spotted you out there." He motioned toward this master suite. "How's the room shaping up?"

She felt both trust and distrust but then she and Quinn were equally guilty of the two emotions.

"It's finished. I'll show you." She hurried to the kitchen,

disposed of the apple core and slid the plate into the dishwasher. When she returned to the family room, she beckoned him to follow.

Her anxiety grew as Quinn neared the room. The suite was his private space, and he'd allowed her to tamper with it. When she arrived at the doorway, she stood back to let him enter first.

From the doorway, she observed Quinn perusing the room. He pointed to the map above the bed. "A nice touch." He wandered to the nightstand and ran his finger down the Belleek castle design of the lamp base. He looked pleased.

She waited, her pulse racing like a stallion.

His eyes shifted to the fireplace, and he crossed to the chair and fingered the Celtic throw she'd tossed over the back. "You did a great job, Ava. It's filled with Irish memories."

Her response skidded when she heard his intake of breath. He turned and spotted the family photos she'd had matted and framed.

Silence pulsed as she waited, motionless and questioning her wisdom or lack of it.

When his hand moved, she followed it to his face where it remained pressed to his cheek. The air filled with palpable tension.

Her head throbbed.

He shifted, and Ava steadied her heart, an apology clinging to her throat.

As he turned, moisture rested on the rim of his eyes.

"Quinn, I thought—"

"Ava, I…" He didn't look at her though he turned away from the pictures.

Reeling, she searched his face, questions storming his mind. "You don't like them."

His eyes downcast, he stood for a moment as if reviewing her question.

"It's not that. They hurt. Badly." He lifted his eyes. "I haven't looked at them since—"

"I'm sorry, Quinn. I thought— I hoped you'd understand why I—"

He finally looked at her. "I know why. I've told you how many times I've changed. I have but seeing the photos...I don't know."

Her chest ached with sadness for his reality and her unthinking action. She expected him to ask her about every decision he made about Brandon, yet she hadn't given him the same respect. "We can take them down, Quinn. I'll have to find something else to put up since I've—"

"See what you can do, okay?" He shook his head. "I don't want Liam and Jen to see the empty picture hangers. It might stir up questions, and I don't want to lie to them."

His reason jarred her. Couldn't he be honest even with his brother? "I don't think there's anything upstairs. We'll have to shop for—"

"Ava. I'm sorry." His expression took her unaware. Surprised. Apologetic.

Her lungs ached. "So am I."

He opened his arms and she stepped into them. His eyes captured hers. "You've done so much for me. I hope you know that."

But not enough. She loosened her arm and swept it to the side, eager to change the subject. "Look what you've done for me. You've let me use a talent that I'd all but buried. I'll always be grateful." She couldn't look at him.

He tilted her chin upward, her eyes still evading his. "Forgive me, Ava. I'm nearly there. Nearly healed. And I owe it all to you."

She managed to look at him, her lungs drawing air as her gaze swept his. Quinn's lips met hers, the kiss deeper than before, his lips exploring hers, his heartbeat in rhythm to the drumming in her head. Despite the disappointment, she recognized the love in his eyes. Weakness wrought her legs useless. She clung to him for stability, joy reverberating through her, a feeling she'd all but lost.

He brushed her cheek with his palm, his gaze tied to hers. "One day I hope you and Brandon will be able to look out over Dingle Bay or stand at the Cliffs of Moher. I'd love you to experience why Ireland is called the Emerald Isle. You'd love it."

One day. Unable to envision or even comprehend his words. He cared about her. He did care. But did he trust her or not?

Quinn heard the doorbell and hurried down the stairs. He wasn't expecting anyone so the sound surprised him. When he looked outside, he saw Ava's car, but instead of her at the door, Brandon grinned at him with something in his hand.

"What's that you got?" He gave a head-toss toward the paper.

Brandon opened it full width and held it in front of him.

He chuckled and gave Brandon a high five. "Finally. The learner's permit."

The teen nodded. "Thanks for giving a good word for me."

It hadn't gone well that day, and he didn't want to think about it, but today spelled success for Brandon. "You're not driving already?" He eyed the car. "Where's your mom?"

He turned toward the car. "She's waiting with Mike. He went with us."

"They can come in. Maybe Mike and you would like to shoot some hoops in celebration."

His face beamed as he bounded down the sidewalk to the driveway.

Quinn used his hand as a megaphone. "Tell your mom I can use her help."

Bran glanced over his shoulder and gave a nod.

Quinn stood on the threshold, hoping she would accept

his invitation. Their last time together clung to his thoughts, and he faced an important realization. While each had the other's best intention at heart, they seemed to use their differences to keep them apart rather than bring them together. That had to change.

Ava had taken a chance that had knocked some sense into him. When he saw the four framed photos she'd hung in his bedroom, he understood her anxiety. She had no idea how he would react. He claimed to be a new man, but he hadn't allowed the healing to be deep enough. He harbored guilt that she said was senseless. Could he have saved his son's life if he'd been behind the wheel?

Though the photos had pierced his heart, the more he studied them, he envisioned Ava and Bran standing in the lovely setting. He realized the Lord had opened a door—allowing him to close the pain of the other one. He would always love Lydia and Sean, but love had no limit. His heart overflowed with the love he still had to give. The time was now to close the door on the past and open wide the new door.

His pulse skipped when he saw Ava open the car door and step out. Mike climbed from the backseat, and the three of them came up the walk. He gave Mike a smile and extended his hand at their introduction. He'd heard a lot about the teen, but this was the first meeting of any of Brandon's friends.

Mike gave his hand a shake, but his eyes shifted from one side to the other, taking in the house. "This place is big."

"Too big for me." He managed a chuckle, but the memory took him back to months ago when he'd first talked with Ross about the vinyl trim and the new roof. Today the house seemed the perfect size.

"We're going outside, okay?" Bran motioned past the staircase to the room beyond.

"Sure." He smiled. "The ball is just inside the garage." As the boys headed off, he grasped Ava's hand. "You couldn't have come at a better time."

A questioning grin touched her face. "Why?"

"My brother's coming tomorrow, remember?"

Her questioning look deepened. "And?"

"He and his wife are staying the night." He motioned toward the second floor. "I'm trying to set up a bedroom."

She gave him a why-didn't-you-tell-me-earlier look. "You're pushing your luck." She swooped past him and climbed the stairs.

Quinn watched her a moment, enjoying the ease with which she took on a task. She'd grown lovelier every day. He took two steps at a time behind her and reached the top at the same time she had.

"This way." He led her across the walkway to the other side, glancing below to admire her handiwork. The living room's green-and-white paint with the splash of yellow and touches of beige gave the room a striking look while the family room she'd left beige with touches of bright earth palette she picked up from the kitchen. He'd admired Lydia's formal decor, but Ava had captured his spirit. "In here." He pointed to the largest bedroom looking out to the front.

She stepped through the doorway and paused. "You set up a bed, I see."

"I couldn't decide what else it needed."

"How about sheets and pillows?" She grinned and sent him on his way. He opened the hall linen closet and pulled out queen-size sheets and located two pillows, and when he returned, Ava had already surprised him.

"This chair was in the other room, and I noticed a table and lamp we can use. I think there's a few pieces of artwork, too."

She vanished through the doorway while he tackled putting linens on the bed. By the time she returned with two scenic oil prints, a throw rug and a bedspread of the same colors, he wondered what he would have done without her. They worked together until the room looked complete.

Ava stood back, as she always did when taking in the decor, scouring the scene. "It needs a few more items to complete the look, but it'll do for tomorrow, I think." Her face brightened. "I can add a vase of flowers from the garden." She touched his arm. "That will look lovely."

He agreed while his head filled with visions of her living in the house. The amazing feeling bored into the empty crevices of his heart. He'd been hollow. He extended his hand, and when she grasped it, he drew her closer. Her frame against his, he drank in the scent of her shampoo and the feel of her smooth skin against his hand. "What would I do without you?"

"Have a quieter life."

He kissed the end of her nose, aware that the boys could come bounding up the stairs any minute. "I like noise."

A sweet smile grew on her lips. "I'm glad."

He turned toward the door, but she placed her hand on his arm. "Can we sit here a minute?"

Her question aroused his curiosity. She sank onto the chair as he settled on the edge of the mattress.

She remained quiet for a moment before she spoke. "We need to talk about a couple of things. First, I haven't had a chance to look for new artwork for the bedroom, but if you—"

His pulse pinged. "No. I've given it thought, Ava."

Her brow wrinkled with question.

"You did the right thing. I give a good talk, but it's time I follow what I'm saying. I tell you I'm different, but until I face the past and close the door, I haven't changed enough. God's given me you. That's all I need."

Her expression remained unchanged, as if she didn't understand.

"We'll leave the photos there. In the past couple of days, I see them differently. They bring back good memories and remind me that I have many more amazing times to come, and better than before because my life isn't focused on the business but on family and the Lord."

When he finished, he noticed tears misting her eyes and he longed to hold her, but knowing she had more to say, he hesitated.

"You couldn't have said anything to make me happier, Quinn. I hoped the photos would be a healing balm, not a deeper hurt."

"I'm slow at some things, Ava. Remember a long time ago, I mentioned a snail's pace. I guess that's me." His spirit lifted with her smile. "But you had something else to tell me?"

A light lit her eyes. "I do, and it's important. I hope it will explain something about me. Maybe I'm a snail, too, Quinn." Her lips curved to a half grin. "I started telling you something more than a week ago, but we were interrupted by Brandon. I thought we'd have a better chance to talk up here without interruption."

He thought back, trying to remember.

"I told you that I had a trust issue, but I never explained." The memory rolled into his mind as his own wavering trust surfaced.

"I don't like talking about this, but I must since it will help you understand something significant about me."

From her expression, he recognized her struggle to be open. How often had he dealt with the same issue? As he listened to her situation with Tom and their financial loss with his pyramid scheme, Quinn's frustration grew. How could a man with a family not discuss something that important with his wife?

As the words came to him, he couldn't say them. He never discussed business with Lydia. She knew nothing about his business, but he acknowledged how well she managed the household. He'd never given her credit, and he'd never offered her a chance to learn more about running the corporation. He realized now she would have been interested.

Ava's gaze sought his. "So anything to do with finances scares me. I question people's motives, and I look askance at money-making ventures. I shouldn't have doubted you."

"I understand, Ava." He braced his hands against the mattress and rose, his hand reaching for hers.

She grasped it, deep sadness in her eyes. "Trust is important in any relationship."

He heard something in her voice, but the subtlety was lost on him. "It is."

She rose, facing him, her eyes probing his. "I'm glad you feel that way."

Before he could follow his heart and kiss her, a noise on the staircase alerted him. He hurried into the hallway as Brandon headed their way. He waylaid him, and they descended the stairs where Mike waited at the bottom. When he looked up, he realized Ava hadn't followed. "Your mom is putting a room together for my brother." He explained the situation as he led the boys into the kitchen. "How about a pop?"

They nodded, and he pulled their choices from the refrigerator. When he handed them the drinks, he motioned them to sit.

Mike gazed around the room and pulled out a chair. "You have a nice house and the best place to play basketball."

"Thanks." He grinned at the boy's wide eyes. "It's good exercise." He needed a reason for putting up the hoop. He joined them at the table. "What happens now with your permit?"

He watched Brandon stroke his pocket as if he carried a gem inside. "I have to drive with a parent or someone over twenty-one."

"Not just anyone." Mike lowered the can to the table. "It has to be someone our parents give permission."

Brandon gave Mike a poke. "You didn't let me finish. And we log our hours. First, I log in thirty hours and a couple hours driving at night. Then we have six more hours of instruction in a classroom, and I can get the Segment 2 permit."

Quinn grinned. "And I know what that means. You're free to drive during the day."

"Right." Brandon grinned and gave him a high five.

Quinn grasped his shoulder and gave it a playful shake. "No night driving yet."

Brandon nodded, giving him a crooked grin.

Though he'd managed to smile and support Brandon, the reality of the situation wrought his senses. He pictured Ava riding in the passenger seat while Bran drove. Quinn remembered the cold facts. Accidents happened. He'd recognized that the day he and Ava met in the ACO parking lot.

"I'll give your mom some help and go with you sometimes."

His eyes became saucers. "Really? You'd do that for me?"

He would do anything for the teen, but the offer stabbed him in the chest. He'd taken Sean out a few times, but Sean's driving riled him. The dark memory hung over him like a storm cloud. He should have been more patient.

Despite his anxiety, Quinn regrouped. "It'll help your mom, and I'd be glad to."

"Glad to what?"

Ava's voice touched a chord. He should have asked her first.

"Quinn offered to take me driving sometimes."

She eyed him, her head tilted as if measuring what she'd heard. "You did?"

Seeing the expression on her face, he cringed inwardly. In her eyes, he'd overstepped his bounds agin. "That is if you don't mind."

Ava didn't answer. She opened the refrigerator and pulled out a can of diet pop.

It gave him time to get a grip and measure how much damage he'd done.

Ava's attitude pierced him as darkly as his own stormy recollection of his behavior with Sean. When would things change between him and Ava? Or should he give up?

Chapter Thirteen

Ava lowered her fork onto the salad plate, taking in the surroundings. She'd heard of Lily's Seafood but never had enough spare money to eat there. The light turquoise-and-coral decor highlighted by oak wood booths and oak flooring gave it a vibrant look. She grinned at the mural that made her think of the man in the moon with a hat.

But her grin slipped away when she looked at Quinn. His offer to ride with Brandon had set her on edge again. How many times would she allow it to happen? After she'd considered his offer, her senses returned. He wanted to help her not interfere. She was sick of her attitude, and she knew Quinn had to be. How much longer would he put up with her? Her disparaging attitude had to change if she had any hope of a permanent relationship with him. Her value as a mother was more than her control over her son. It had to do with trust, faith and love. Why couldn't she open her heart to that?

She forced her mind back to the conversation. Liam and Quinn looked like brothers with similar features, both good-looking men. Their differences showed in their personalities. Liam had a tougher exterior. She noticed him scrutinize her numerous times when he thought she wasn't looking.

"It was nice meeting your son this afternoon." Jen's voice cut through Ava's thoughts.

"Quinn wanted him to meet you, so we came up with the picnic lunch idea. I enjoy the garden area. It's a beautiful setting." She pictured the lovely afternoon as they enjoyed the sun and celebrated her birthday. "Thanks for making my birthday special."

"You're welcome. And your son gave you the prettiest bracelet."

Ava controlled her grin, certain that Quinn had helped with the bracelet.

"And I can see he thinks the world of Quinn."

Ava saw it, too. She remembered only a few months ago when she and Bran were nose to nose in daily arguments. "Thank you. He's becoming a man, and I'm relieved that he's found a friend in Quinn."

"Your husband died?"

Jen's compassionate voice touched her. "Yes, when Bran was twelve."

"A long illness?" Jen gave her a quizzical look.

"No." She explained Tom's death. "He was gone quickly." She drew back. "Very difficult."

With sympathy growing on her face, Jen quieted for a moment while Ava caught snatches of the brothers' business talk. According to their business conversation, Quinn took charge and could be hard-nosed. She couldn't picture it.

In moments, Jen returned to her questions—what did she do for a living, did she live far from Quinn and would Brandon stay in remission. She wished she knew the answer. The woman seemed to have a penchant for asking probing questions and Ava almost chuckled thinking of the many people who accused her of doing the same.

When she finished answering Jen's questions and asked a few of her own, her thoughts slipped back to the afternoon. Liam had asked his share of questions, too, and she sensed his curiosity about her. Quinn hadn't blinked an eye while pulling the conversation in other directions and giving his brother a subtle frown, but Ava caught it.

She supposed it was typical of a man to size up a new woman in his brother's life. Love camouflaged flaws until it was too late. She thought back to her earlier concern, but today as she listened to the men talk, she recognized the complexities of his business, and she knew she'd been very wrong to think otherwise.

When Jen rested her hand on Ava's arm, she pulled herself from her musing. Jen gave her an apologetic look. "Sorry. I made you jump."

"I was thinking about this afternoon." And so much more.

Jen nodded. "I'm glad we could be here to celebrate. I want you to know, Ava, that I like you a lot. I can see why Quinn thinks so much of you."

Her pulse skipped hearing Jen's observation. "He's been very kind."

Jen arched an eyebrow. "It's more than kindness. I'm sure you realize that."

She feared letting her mind and heart agree. The emotions led to vulnerability, and it scared her. She'd prided herself on being self-sufficient, yet she'd already given in and allowed Quinn to take over her life. No, to fill her life.

"You've done a magnificent job at the house. I love the colors you used and the way you brought a sense of connection to the rooms. You're very talented."

Ava's worry faded. She'd been concerned about Liam's attitude toward her, but Jen liked her, and that was more important. Women bonded in a special way, sometimes only a feeling in the heart. She sensed she could be open with Jen. "I would love to do home design for a living, but I married young and I'm not trained."

"No one would ever know, Ava. You have a God-given skill." She gazed at Quinn a moment, and as if a light came on inside her, her face glowed. "Quinn could set you up. He's a wonderful businessman, and he knows the ropes. I'm sure word of mouth would keep you busy when people see what you've done at Quinn's."

Though her pride mounted, thinking of running her own business set her imagination flying. "Thanks for the validation, but Quinn has very few visitors. I doubt word of mouth would work for this situation."

"I hope that changes when you and he..." Her glow dimmed as she pressed her lips together. "I think I've said too much, but I can see you two as a couple. I've never seen Quinn as happy."

Ava's heart stirred at Jen's admission. Quinn had said the same.

Jen leaned closer speaking near her ear. "I don't know how much you know about Quinn, but business came first. He turned his company into an international corporation. A huge success. He's shrewd but honest. I admire that in him."

International. Success. Honest. Her earlier speculation about him seemed to vanish. Ashamed even more at her accusations, Ava managed to swallow her confession as to her earlier conjecture. Quinn could have walked away from her for her lack of trust.

Jen leaned in again. "I was surprised when Liam told me Quinn had renovated the house. We knew he'd purchased a smaller home—he showed us photographs—and though it was attractive, he stunned us when he sold his gorgeous place in Grand Rapids."

Ava's heart plunged to her stomach, the beat so strong she couldn't think.

"Six bedrooms and baths, lovely living room, music room with Lydia's grand piano, dining room fit for a queen, servants' quarters, although Lydia wouldn't hear of live-in help. She did hire a cleaning lady and had a chef who came in for special occasions." She drew back, a startled expression on her face. "Whoa. I haven't let you say a word."

Words were lost. Ava's mind reeled with all she'd learned. She managed to put her astonishment to rest. "I've enjoyed listening. Quinn's private and doesn't talk much about himself. But he's opening up, and it's as if he's spoon-feeding me with tidbits of his life with Lydia and Sean."

"Devastating. That's all I can say."

Ava looked down and realized the waiter had slipped the entreé in front of her without her noticing. She'd tried to order the chicken dish, less expensive than most everything on the menu, but Quinn insisted she try the chargrilled Northern Atlantic salmon. The price startled her, but after the first taste she was glad she did. Her taste buds tingled with the savory mustard sauce with a touch of tarragon. Quinn's king crab platter looked scrumptious, its plump meat sending out a hint of garlic.

The four quieted as they enjoyed the excellent food. She had never experienced so many delicacies on one menu. Liam sent her a smile, and she grinned back wondering if the smile had meaning. He and Quinn had been head to head discussing business, but occasionally she noticed their focus on her and Jen. If she didn't pass his inspection, Jen had given her a stamp of approval and she hoped that counted.

Quinn slid his plate back and patted his belly. "Save room for dessert. This is the place that takes Royal Oakers down memory lane."

She had no idea what he was talking about, and she suspected Liam and Jen didn't, either. "What?"

He chuckled. "Wait. You'll see."

She shook her head, enjoying his lightheartedness. They'd spent so much time in stress-mode that learning to relax seemed a gift.

"I hear Quinn's buying your son a car."

Liam's voice startled her. She turned toward him, trying

to control her discomfort. "No, he's not. He offered but I said no."

Liam's eyebrow arched. "Why?"

"It's up to me to provide a vehicle for my son, but I appreciated Quinn's generous offer."

Quinn sought her gaze, his eyes apologetic. But his look changed when he turned to Liam. "My plan was to hire Brandon to work in the yard for the summer. He said he'd like to save for a car, and the job would help him pay for it."

Liam leaned back and chuckled. "That's a lot of lawn work, but I'm glad to hear he wants to save. Shows he knows the value of hard work."

Ava's tension eased. "Thanks, I'm proud of him."

Jen nodded. "Especially with what he's been through."

Liam agreed and rubbed his hands together. "Now, I think it's time we celebrate Ava's birthday."

"I agree." Quinn smiled and slipped his hand into his jacket pocket, pulling out a small jewelry box. His eyes searched hers. "This is a good time to give you this."

Quinn placed the box in her palm, her heart fluttering with hummingbird wings.

"Open it." He sent her a silly grin. "You notice I'm not good at wrapping."

She studied the small box, her heart in her throat. "This is quite a surprise."

Jen gave her a nudge. "Open it. I can't wait."

Neither could she. She lifted the lid and lying on the bed of velvet was a gold chain, glinting as if it were made of diamonds, and holding a pendant. She lifted it out, gazing at the unique design, two hands clasping a heart and resting under a crown. "It's lovely, Quinn. I've never seen anything like it."

"That's because it's Irish. The design is called a Claddagh. They're very popular there." He opened his hand. "Would you like me to clasp it for you?"

She nodded, handing him the necklace and lifting her short

hair so he could place it around her neck. The pendant lay in the V-neckline of her dress, and she fingered the design. "It's beautiful. Thank you so much."

As if the waiter had been watching, he appeared with a tray filled with cream puffs and chocolate topping. Jen gave the dessert a quizzical look. "How does this take you down memory lane?"

"The topping is Saunder's Hot Fudge. They had an ice-cream shop on Fourth Street, and everyone flocked there for their cream puff filled with French vanilla ice cream and topped with their famous hot fudge."

"Not to mention the whipped cream and cherry." Jen plucked off the fruit and popped it in her mouth.

Ava grinned at Jen's playfulness and then faced her own plate. Liam and Quinn dug into the dessert while she and Jen only nibbled. When Jen lowered her spoon, she leaned closer to her again. "Do you know about the Claddagh design?" Her voice was a whisper.

"No." But curious, Ava eyed Jen's I-told-you-so expression.

Jen's face blossomed to a full smile. "Each element of the design is a symbol. The two hands represent friendship, the heart they're clasping is for love and the crown symbolizes loyalty."

"Everyone knows this?" Ava's heart thundered.

"Most people, I'm sure. It's especially important to people in love." Jen gave her a little poke.

People in love. The words wound through Ava's mind, and she wondered if Quinn realized the meaning.

Quinn looked up as Jen entered the kitchen. "Did you sleep well?"

"After a while, but it wasn't the bed's fault. It was Liam." She pulled out a chair, sat and folded her hands on the table. "He'd been so suspicious about Ava, and then he did a hundred-eighty-degree turn. I was thrilled. She's a good woman, Quinn."

"I know, and I was glad to hear him say what he did. Although I listened to his concerns—he's my brother, you know—I never agreed with him. I knew he'd change once he met Ava." Quinn stood. "How about some coffee?"

"Thanks. A little cream or milk, please."

He prepared her coffee and set it in front of her. "Ava would impress anyone. She fought her own battles and survived without help from anyone."

"She impressed me. Ava's a gem." The darkness brightened to a coy grin. "Your gift didn't pass by me without reading the message. You are smitten. Am I right?"

Though uneasy admitting the truth, Quinn nodded. "But I haven't told her yet."

"She'd be blind if she didn't know." She shook her head with a laugh. "I think the Claddagh was an obvious hint."

"She said she'd never heard of the symbol." His heart skipped, seeing Jen's expression. "You told her."

"What did you want me to do? Keep her in the dark?" She rose from the chair and kissed his cheek.

"Good morning." Liam came through the archway and eyed them.

Jen turned and embraced him, planting a quick kiss on his lips. "You caught us." She tousled his neatly combed hair.

Liam ran his fingers through it as if they were a comb. He opened two cabinets before he found the cups and poured his coffee. When he turned back, Quinn spotted an apology in his eyes. "I really like Ava, Quinn. I was very wrong, and I hope you can forgive me for my earlier scrutiny."

"Apology accepted. Now, sit and tell me what you really think."

Liam took a sip of his coffee and stared at the tabletop. "I like her." He looked Quinn in the eyes. "I had a preconceived notion that a woman without much might see dollar signs and not the man. I was totally wrong. Her attitude, along with everything she said last night, set me straight. She's a strong, capable woman."

Quinn couldn't help but grin. "She's as honest and direct as they come." Quinn remembered their meeting, her probing questions, her straightforwardness. Those were things he learned to love about her.

"I found her delightful." Jen's comment was the first since Liam had come into the room. "And what a talented woman. Look at the love in these rooms."

Liam gazed around the room. "She is talented."

Quinn's chest swelled, recalling Ava's enthusiasm and creativity throughout her work there. "We have a couple of hurdles to get over, but soon I hope I can tell her how I feel."

"Hurdles?" Jen slipped into the chair beside him.

He gave them a brief version of their tension with his relationship with Brandon and his involvement with Dreams Come True. The issues seemed so trivial when he said them, but he knew both dealt with trust. She had to trust her role as Brandon's mother and he had to trust her with his secret.

"Why not back off a little with Brandon? Focus more on her."

Jen's words wove through his mind. "I do focus on her, but Brandon is a big part of our lives." His offer bumped through his mind. "I told Brandon I'd take him out for driving practice, and I can't withdraw that now."

Liam slid his mug back and forth on the table. "Does Ava know?"

"She has a hard time letting go of being the only one Brandon can count on." He swallowed. "But I have them, too. I picture Sean and…"

Jen released a quiet sob. "It's difficult, Quinn. They're the same age as when—" She erased her words with her hand. "But I can see good in it, too."

"So can I." The honest admission surprised him. "I need

to be the kind of father I should have been with Sean. I've made valiant efforts to grow, to change. At least, I'm trying." He swung his arm out embracing the rooms. "You can see the difference, I hope. And I'm happy."

"That's what counts." Liam's voice came from the back of his throat as if he, too, were struggling with emotion. "I see the difference. You've never smiled so much."

"And it's deep." He rested his hand on his chest. "It's not just about me and the business. It's about life, people I care about and the Lord. It's been a long time before I made peace with a God I knew loved me, but I doubted."

Liam stood and drew Quinn into an embrace. Brother to brother, they stood together in a kind of friendship they had never experienced. Forgiveness was not a question. Liam cared about him and that's all that counted.

Chapter Fourteen

Quinn stood outside the church, watching for Ava. Afte[r] the service, he'd promised to take Brandon out to driv[e] but foremost he wanted to apologize for his brother's gri[pp]ing during the afternoon of her birthday. With his broth[er] there, he hadn't had a chance to talk with her, but now h[e] had time. Liam and Jen didn't head home until he was lea[v]ing for church.

When he saw the dark red sedan pull into the parking lo[t] he headed her way. Brandon saw him first and gave a wav[e]. Whenever he saw the teen since he'd gotten his learner[s] permit, his pulse escalated, his memories running rampan[t]. He prayed daily Brandon would have no mishaps in the ca[r]. Now he needed to trust the Lord to answer his prayer.

His fears were ridiculous. Well-seasoned drivers died i[n] car crashes daily. Experience and expertise held no gua[r]antee that accidents wouldn't happen. Today would test hi[s] ability to allow Brandon to drive without his negative com[m]ents at each imperfection at the wheel. He had to give th[e] boy a chance.

Brandon's grin greeted him from a distance, and Ava gav[e] a wave. He studied her expression hoping it rang true to th[e] greeting.

"Hi." He grasped Brandon's shoulder and gave it a squeeze while slipping his hand behind Ava's back without being obvious. He wondered if the boy recognized their attraction. "Ready for your driving practice?"

"Yep, I'm stoked."

Quinn wished he could say the same. "We'll head out after fellowship. You can hang with your buddies for a little while. Okay?"

Brandon shrugged. "Sure."

The delay obviously didn't stoke him. Quinn hid his grin and said in a lowered voice to Ava, "I hope we have a little time to talk. I want to explain—"

"If you're talking about Liam, no need."

He hesitated a moment with her comment. "Yes, there is. Cooperation, remember?"

That made her grin. "I mean it. I liked them both."

Her unexpected smile ended his concern.

The music began and the spirit of the songs sent Quinn's toes tapping, but during the readings and a testimony, his mind sought a different path while he struggled to stay focused. The question of his feelings for Ava had plagued him since they first met. He'd been drawn to her without reason. She intrigued him, and he chalked it up to admiration to all she'd gone through alone and still remained strong.

But time had moved on, and his admiration branched off to deeper feelings. Admiration remained part of it, but she delighted him. She taught him things about himself. Her quirky questions, the probing he disliked, became a comfort. The attribute defined her curiosity and added to her creativity.

And now the trust factor remained. Each had issues. Each of them needed to grow and to accept. God's Word had opened their minds and broadened their views on life…and on love. He'd thought love had died with his family, but he'd learned the amazing limitlessness of God's greatest commandment. To love. Love grew and spread. It couldn't be boxed or buried.

His chest ached with the spiraling awareness. With the Lord's help, he, Ava and Brandon could be whole again...if they would allow God to work in their hearts.

The music captured his attention again, and he roused from his thoughts to join in the singing. As the service concluded, Brandon vanished with a friend, and Quinn walked beside Ava, both silent, as they headed for the coffee hour. Today he hoped Ross and Kelsey wouldn't seek them out. He and Ava needed time alone.

"Hey."

When he heard Kelsey's voice, his stomach sank.

Ava slowed and moved to the side, waiting for Kelsey, but he strode away, thinking it might speed their conversation. Instead, Kelsey hailed him back. Disappointed, he smoothed his frown and faced her. "You wanted me?"

She grinned. "Both of you."

He and Ava glanced at each other before turning their attention to Kelsey.

"I have a friend who's looking for someone to do some interior design in her home. She's not looking for a Candice Olson."

Ava chuckled but he had no idea what that meant.

Kelsey must have noticed. "She's a leading designer with a TV show."

He gave her a helpless shrug, and she grinned. "I told my friend about what you've done at Quinn's and Ross says what he saw is great. And don't forget, I've seen your house. So, Quinn, would you mind if she gives you a call? She'd like to see what Ava's accomplished."

He eyed Ava, and she looked as surprised as he was. "It's fine with me, but it's more up to Ava." He caught her eye. "Do you want to do another decorating job?"

"I love doing it. You know that." Though she said the

words, her self-confidence appeared to falter. "But you need to tell her I'm not a professional. I just seem to have a knack."

"She knows, and I'll come with her because I want to take a look, too." Her face lit up. "I've been wanting to redo a couple of rooms, and…" She rolled her eyes. "I can talk about that later." She pointed behind her. "Ross is waiting for me in the car. We're meeting Lexie and Ethan for lunch with the kids."

Quinn's lungs refilled. "Okay, have her call me." He took a step and then swung back. "Do you have my phone number?"

"I'll get it from Ava."

He gave a nod and watched her head out before he and Ava continued toward the fellowship hall. "Are you surprised?"

"Sort of." She shook her head. "I'm a little nervous, but I'm excited."

Stoked. Brandon's expression popped into his head. "You can do it, Ava. You had no problem with my place, and dragging my likes and dislikes and interests out of me took extra work."

She arched an eyebrow. "True."

Once they found seats, Quinn tackled the situation with his brother. "I know Liam acted strange. He's a good guy—"

She touched his hand. "He was protecting you. I'm a woman of little means, and apparently…" She grinned and shook her head. "You are a wealthy man, Quinn. I had no idea. Your home is lovely, but for a man volunteering to buy cars and pay repairs and hire plumbers and all the things you've done for us, my mind kept asking, 'What is he doing in Royal Oak? He should be living in Bloomfield Hills or one of those mansions on Lake Shore Drive.'"

"I had one of those in Grand Rapids, Ava."

Her eyes captured his. "I know. Jen told me on Friday."

His pulse skipped, wondering what else she told him. "I have different values now, and I still like nice things but

I'd rather focus on the treasures in heaven than the ones earth."

"I understand, but God rewarded you with those gifts, a He wants you to have a good life, too."

"I do." His heart swelled with her caring thought. "A you're part of it."

"Thank you." She evaded his eyes. "Jen told me so other things, too."

His chest constricted. "What?"

She grinned. "She said she liked me a lot, and she sai had a God-given talent."

The longing to hold her in his arms overwhelmed hi He managed to control the urge and to take her hand in h "Liam likes you, too."

Her head snapped up. "He does? I'm glad."

"Who could help it?"

"Quinn?"

He let his hand slip from Ava's and focused on Brand "Ready?"

Brandon nodded. "My friends are leaving and I'm getti bored."

Quinn rose and slipped his arm around the boy's should "I wouldn't want you to be bored." Though he had more say to Ava, he felt relieved. He studied her face hoping s knew he had more to tell her. "I'll drop him home when we done."

"Stay for dinner?"

He gazed at her tender grin. "I'd love to." He gave he wave as he and Brandon strode to the parking lot.

Beside the SUV passenger door, he dug out his keys a handed them to the teen. "You know what you're doing?"

"I've driven hours on the range and on the highway. learned all the traffic laws. I'm ready." He glowed as he cepted the keys, hit the unlock button and slipped into t driver's seat. He pulled out a small notepad and jotted the time. "You'll have to sign this when I'm done."

"Fine with me." Quinn buckled up, managing to keep a calm demeanor no matter what was going on in his mind.

Brandon had no problem leaving the parking lot, and when they were on the highway, Quinn was pleased he'd started the driving experience on a Sunday. Traffic was lighter, and he drew in a calming breath, but as they approached the traffic lights, Quinn's foot pressed against the floorboard. "Have you had experience on the freeway?"

"A little."

"Let's head north on I-75 for a while, then we'll come back on the highway." No lights on the freeway. His plan made him grin.

As time passed, Quinn knew Brandon had learned good driving techniques. He used his mirrors as he changed lanes, and he followed the speed limit which was more than Quinn could say for himself. Though his confidence grew, Quinn's worries still hovered in the background.

When they left the freeway and started back on the main roads, Quinn's tense posture eased. He arched his back to relieve the strain, and when they were within a mile of Ava's, an idea struck him. "Slow down a little. There's a florist near here, I think."

"You want to buy flowers?" Brandon glanced his way.

"It's a hostess gift. Your mom invited me to dinner."

"The garden's full of flowers. You could pick some."

Quinn chuckled. "Girls like flowers from a florist. You'll learn."

Brandon gave a one-shoulder shrug, and when the Fields Florist sign appeared, Quinn pointed to the sign. Brandon pulled into the parking lot.

Inside Quinn selected a bouquet, pastel flowers the clerk identified as lilies, Gerbera daisies and the one type he knew well—roses. While she arranged them in a vase, he gazed through the window studying Brandon behind the wheel. He'd often reviewed how he and Ava had changed, but he'd overlooked Brandon's growth. He'd mellowed, and instead of the sarcastic teen he'd met two months earlier, the boy had stretched to adulthood.

His last illness may have brought out a more serious side of Brandon. The mono had diminished his energy like a dying battery. But he'd perked up and seemed closer to normal. Spending more time with him piqued Quinn's curiosity, and questions.

"Here you go."

Quinn stepped away from the storefront window and approached the woman holding the bouquet wrapped in floral paper.

"That will be forty-two dollars and thirty-nine cents."

He dug into his wallet and pulled out his credit card. After signing the receipt, he headed back to the car.

When he opened the door, Brandon's eyes were as large as the Gerbera daisies. "That's huge."

"Your mom's worth it, don't you think?" Quinn slipped into the seat and held the bouquet in his hands.

The teen grinned. "She's a good mom. Her life has been devoted to me, and at first I was jealous that you took her time, but she's happier now than I've ever seen her."

Warmth rolled through Quinn. "She's happy because you're doing so well, too."

His expression changed, and an icy feeling overtook the warmth he'd felt. "What's wrong?"

"Nothing." He turned the key in the ignition and backed from the parking spot.

"Don't tell me nothing, Bran. I can tell something's bothering you." He searched the boy's profile, observing his tensed jaw and his evasive expression.

"It's nothing, and I don't want to worry my mom."

Quinn's chest constricted. "What is it? The mono?" He searched his face. "Hodgkin's?"

"Promise you won't run to my mom if I tell you?"

Stifling his first thought, Quinn froze with the question. How could he not tell Ava if it were something serious? Yet how could he reject the boy's offer to tell him? Weighing both choices, he took the one that made more sense. "Let me put it this way." He sucked in air. "I won't run to her with what you're saying, but I can't promise I won't do something about it if I think it's serious."

Brandon's eyes remained on the traffic, but his expression registered his struggle.

"Bran, we'll talk it over before anything is done. I promise."

"It's a lymph node. I think it's left over from the mono, but it's one of the places I had a problem with Hodgkin's so I'm not sure."

His pained expression ripped at Quinn's heart. "Why haven't you told your mom? She loves you so much, and you know she'd—"

"It's in my groin."

Quinn frowned. "And you're not comfort—"

"When I was a boy, it was okay, but I'm a man, and—"

"I understand." His mind steeped with possibilities. Could it be the Hodgkin's? Yes. But it could easily be a swollen gland left from the mono. Give him the benefit of the… No. The quicker he did something… Quinn's head spun.

The turn signal ticked, and he realized Brandon had reached Blair Street. He had to make a decision.

Brandon's jaw ticked as he waited for traffic to clear. "I shouldn't have told you."

"No, Bran. You should have." He sent up a prayer. "Here's what we'll do. Let's wait another week. If it's the mono, it should get smaller or go away altogether."

The car rolled into the driveway.

"Will you be honest with me if it's no better?" Quinn held his breath.

Brandon shifted into Park and pulled out the keys. "I don't have much of a choice, do I?"

"You do, but it could leave you with serious consequences."

Brandon handed him the keys and pushed open his door. "Then I don't have a choice."

Quinn couldn't argue, and he was glad Brandon realized it. He lifted the bouquet and headed inside.

Ava heard the car door and hurried to the window. Brandon rose from the driver's seat all in one piece, and her worry turned to relief. When she noticed Quinn, her heart tripped. Flowers. She stepped to the doorway, trying to keep her gaze from the bouquet. "How did it go?" His expression caused her concern. "Problems?"

"No." He held his arms out at his sides. "We're here. No damage."

"I see that."

"He did very well," Quinn said, extending the bouquet. "These are for you."

She managed to keep from grinning like a kid at Christmas. "What's this for?"

"You invited me to dinner, remember?"

"How could I forget?" She motion him inside, and as she did, her memory spiked. "Bran, Mike called."

Brandon swung back through the doorway. "Did he say what he wanted?"

"His family's going out to dinner for pizza, and you're invited."

His gloomy expression brightened. "Can I go?"

"I don't see why not. I made a big pot roast so there'll be leftovers."

Quinn sniffed the air. "I thought I smelled something good. Roast is one of my favorites."

Brandon vanished into his room as she scooted into the kitchen and unwrapped the bouquet. The beautiful flowers heightened her senses. She drew in the lovely scent of roses and touched the soft petals. When she looked up, Quinn watched her from the doorway. "Can you imagine how long it's been since I've received a bouquet of flowers?"

He gave a quick shake of the head.

"Neither can I." But she could. She'd been surrounded by flowers at Tom's funeral. She brushed the sad thought away. "Thanks. They're gorgeous."

He closed the distance between them as Brandon appeared in the hallway outside the kitchen. "Mike's folks are leaving now. I'm going out front to wait for them."

She wiggled her fingers his way. "Have fun."

He vanished, then popped his head around the corner again. "Thanks, Quinn, for taking me out to drive."

"You're welcome, Bran. You tallied an hour and fifteen minutes, and you did great."

Hearing the bang of the door, Ava relaxed. When Brandon was around, she worried Quinn might forget and touch her hand or give her a hug. He did it so naturally when they were alone. She wondered if Bran suspected they'd become more than friends.

"Dinner will be ready shortly." She gave a head toss. "But first, I want to put these on the living-room table. They're beautiful, and the vase is lovely."

He followed behind her as she stood a moment to decide the best spot to display his thoughtful gift. She set the vase on the table near the front window. Perfect. As she turned, she noticed a strained expression on his face. "What happened?"

Quinn's head bolted upward. "What do you mean?"

"Something went on while you were gone. I expected Bran to come in with details of his first driving practice, but I had to drag it out of him, and though you're smiling, I know you well enough to see that you're upset. Something happened?"

His eyes searched hers a moment, and she longed to be inside his mind to know the truth. To know what had happened. "Quinn?"

He blinked, his focus jumping from her to the window to the floor, until his eyes met hers. "To be honest, this was difficult for me."

The reality struck her. "You thought about Sean."

"Yes, but even more, I remembered how I begrudged every hour I spent on the highway. I expected too much, and I rode him the whole time."

"Why?"

"That was me then. Perfection." He shook his head and caved into an easy chair. "If he didn't brake at the time I would have, I told him. If he shifted lanes, I criticized his use of the mirrors. I'm sure he looked. He never hit anyone, but I had to control him." A look crossed his face that she understood. "Sounds familiar, doesn't it?"

She couldn't deny it. "He did well?"

"Excellent. I was proud of him."

"I'm glad."

His expression eased as his eyes captured hers. He rose and drew her into his arms. "Oops." He stepped away and took a couple of steps to the window. "They just pulled up." He waited a moment, then turned with a smile. "Gone." He rubbed his hands together. "Now, let's get back to our conversation."

His arms opened, and she stepped into his embrace. He drew her close, his hand pressing her to his chest, his mouth seeking hers. Her heart sang to the rhythm of their syncopated heartbeats. When his lips left hers, he kissed her cheek and then her nose. "I see you're wearing the Claddagh necklace."

Her fingers rose, touching the beautiful gift. "I love it. It's special to me since it's Irish, and I know your heritage means a lot to you."

"You mean a lot to me. Do you know that?"

His eyes captured hers and she could only nod.

"Jen said she explained the symbolism."

She nodded again.

"You're not upset with me?"

Adrenaline kicked in as heat spread through her body. "Upset? Why would I be?"

He searched her eyes. "Friendship. Loyalty."

She nodded as he spoke each word.

"Love."

He'd knocked the wind out of her. She searched his eyes. "I know we've sort of grown on each other over the past couple of months." The "but" hung on the air. Love? Her feelings overpowered her, but she'd always thought it took years to fall in love.

He cupped her cheek in his palm. "You think love is too strong? I know it's been only months, but you're on my mind every moment of the day."

"And I think of you all the time." She struggled to form words that expressed what she meant. "We both need time to let the reality sink in. We're still dealing with adjustments, and—"

"We'll be doing that forever." He tilted his head and gazed into her eyes. "Don't you think? We'll learn something new each day. Relationships are discovery."

She lowered her head, knowing what he said made sense. But solid relationships also meant being honest, and she'd been negligent. "Speaking of learning something new each day, are you ready? I need to make a confession."

A frown flickered beneath his tender expression.

She wrapped her mind around the truth. Telling him shouldn't be difficult, but it was. "Okay, I'm just going to say it. The day you ran into me…" She searched his eyes.

"I remember."

"You didn't do it. I ran into you. My bumper dente your quarter panel. No way was it your fault."

His scowl grew to a silly grin. He shook his head. "I k that. It was more fun letting you be deluded." He capt her again—mind, body and emotion—with a kiss that tu her into a pool of melted butter.

Chapter Fifteen

Quinn stepped aside and invited the three women into the house. Kelsey introduced her friend Megan, and Ava's face glowed with anticipation. His own pride reached a peak when Megan and Kelsey let out an "ohhh" when they stepped into the living room. He hovered in the hallway, listening to their comments about the color scheme. He grinned, marveling at Ava's understanding design without training. This was what she was meant to do.

Uneasy about being caught eavesdropping, he strode into the kitchen and settled at the bay window breakfast nook, gazing outside at the garden. The work Ava and Bran had accomplished had turned a weed patch into a colorful display of flowers. He'd helped with the trimming, but Ava's creativity put a special touch to the landscaping. She had more plans, but he'd convinced her to wait until next year or autumn when they could plant bulbs to come up in the spring. If he left it all to her, she would have created another garden of Versailles.

The women's voices drew closer and then faded. He suspected they'd gone into his bedroom. He wished he could be there to listen, but he stayed put. Soon they had reached the family room where the conversation reverberated into the kitchen.

Ava's voice sparkled with enthusiasm. "Although the d
is traditional, I added Quinn's personal style. You saw
Irish influence in his bedroom suite, and throughout y
see his love of nature in the color palette, both here and i
kitchen. I also added an urban flavor with the brilliant j
tones. The decorative items such as the fabrics and fra
prints also bring the outside in."

From the nook, he saw her pass the doorway, and
wanted to hug her.

Ava opened the outside door. "This beveled door lea
the patio. I also worked on the landscaping. Would you
to see it?"

Eager voices agreed, and they vanished outside. Whil
watched them wander between the flowerbeds, his cell p
jingled. He pulled it from his pocket, surprised to see the
came from Ava's house. He pushed the button. "What's
pening, Bran?"

The silence disturbed him. "Brandon, what's wrong?

"Can't you guess?" His downhearted voice sliced thr
Quinn.

His pulse skipped. "Did you get in an accident?"

"No. My mom has the car."

Quinn knew that, but he might have been driving w
friend. Grateful that he could cross off an accident, the
concern caught him off guard. "The swelling?"

"What else?" Silence again. "It's still there. Not sma
but I don't think bigger, either."

Quinn glanced out the window, worried the women w
return. He rose and strode through the kitchen into the di
room. "You know what you have to do."

"I guess."

"No. There's no guessing. You must tell your mom." Q
dragged air into his lungs.

"She's not home. I don't know where she is."

His chest ached. "She's here, showing off her decora

to a couple of ladies." He released the stream of air. "You'll have to tell her when she gets home."

Silence.

"I know it's not easy, but it needs to be looked at just to make sure. It's necessary."

"Could you come over? Maybe if you're here—"

He could easily cave in hearing the boy's plea. "Think about it, Bran." He imagined Ava's resentment. "I think you should be alone when you tell her. My being there won't make it easier."

A long silence stretched on the line before Brandon spoke. "If you think so."

"I do, but you know I'll be with you all the way. I'm praying right now that it's nothing serious. That's what you need to do, too. You know that?"

"I know."

No brilliant response came to him. "Good. Prayer is best right now."

The women's voices grew louder from the kitchen. "Your mom is coming this way. I'll talk with you later."

Brandon hung up, and Quinn sank into a dining-room chair, wondering what to do now. He had to get his wits about him. Ava seemed to read every nuance on his face. If she knew he'd been involved before Brandon told her, she wouldn't handle it well at all, he feared.

Ava drove away from Quinn's house, her heart in her throat. Megan seemed impressed, but how she really felt was only a guess.

"Quinn's house is gorgeous." Kelsey leaned toward her from the backseat. "And you did a tremendous job. I hadn't seen it before, but I remember your saying the last owners liked beige."

Megan chuckled. "I think a lot of us want to be safe. My house has lots of beige, but I'm telling you, Ava, I love what

you did. The color choices were amazing. The kitchen a
the family room glowed like a sunset. Yet the master s
sent out calm vibes like a spring rain."

Kelsey chuckled. "Aren't you poetic."

"I guess that's what the decor did to me, and the hous
amazing. I would guess the upstairs has numerous bedroo
too."

"Four and two bathrooms." She slowed for a red li
"Quinn said one day he wanted to do some things up th
but right now he has no reason."

Kelsey gave the back of her seat a poke. "Right now,
you never know."

Megan did a quick turn. "Is this a romance?"

Ava swallowed, her hand rising to the Claddagh pend
"Only a mini one."

The women laughed and settled to silence while Ava
lived Quinn's last conversation with her. The word love
come into play, and though it roused her heartbeat to a ga
the actuality set her on edge. She'd never dreamed of fall
in love again, and now that Brandon's health remained sta
the doors had opened. But any day bad news could dar
her door again. How would she have time for a romance
a son dealing with cancer?

"I'm very interested in your taking a look at my hou
Ava."

Megan's voice cut through her musing, and she too
moment to rouse herself. "I'd love to see it. I'd want to kr
about your interests and lifestyle. Take notes of your fl
plan and get an idea of your budget."

"I convinced my husband we needed to refurbish
house. He seemed agreeable, but we didn't talk dollars
cents."

"No need until I take a look."

"Great. Let's pick out a time before you head over.
make sure the place is clean."

They chuckled again, but Ava's mind drifted far from house cleaning. The thought of having a real career—one she would love and be proud of—tore through her mind.

When she'd dropped the women at Kelsey's and said good-bye, she headed home, anxious to call Quinn and tell him what happened. He'd suggested she had talent for a career. So did Jen, but she didn't believe either of them. Another doubting moment.

She floated into the house on clouds, her mind soaring with ideas she'd kept locked into her secret place of wishes. But she knew dreams could come true. The phrase jolted her again. She longed to talk to Quinn about her speculation, but she'd caused a ruckus with her off-the-wall pyramid scheme. She'd hurt him. Suggesting another of her cockamamy suppositions might be another "straw that broke the camel's back" situation. Right now she wanted no part of it.

She walked through the house to the kitchen, looking for Brandon. He usually plunked himself in front of the TV when he was bored, but not today. "Bran?"

Heading toward his room, she paused noticing the closed door. Concern rippled down her back. "Bran? Are you busy?"

She stood a moment, waiting for his response, but before he spoke, she noticed the doorknob turn, and Brandon looked at her. He looked upset, and her first thought was an accident.

"Bran, did you get in an acci—"

"Quinn asked me the same thing." He paled as the words left him.

"Quinn? Did you talk with him?"

His eyes shifted toward the window and back again. "I thought he might know where you were."

She didn't believe him. "Then you knew I was there."

He nodded.

"Do you want me to come in there, or are you coming out?" Something horrible happened, no matter what he said. She stepped back, waiting for his response.

He shrugged and stepped out of his room.

Ava let him lead, and she followed him into the liv
room where he plopped on the sofa. He tossed his head b.
against the cushion, and she stood watching him, waiting
him to break the bad news.

He finally straightened up and looked at her. "Aren't
going to sit?"

"Should I?"

He shook his head. "I have a swollen lymph node in
groin."

Air escaped her lungs. "No." She shook her head, alm
wishing he'd dented her car or scraped the door. Not can
again. "What about the mono? Could it be that?"

He looked downtrodden. "It's been two months.
other swelling is gone." He shook his head. "Mom, I d
know."

"Then we'll call Dr. Franklin's office right now and m.
an appointment." She rose and made the call, relieved they
ranged an appointment date sooner than she expected. W
she hung up, she returned to Brandon. "He can see you
Tuesday. That's only four days from now."

He looked devastated, and his expression tugged on
heart, but at the same time, she hadn't forgotten his re
ence to Quinn. "You told Quinn about your problem w
you called."

He nodded, guilt spread across his face.

"Why didn't he tell me?"

"He said I should tell you. He knew you'd be worried.
made me promise last week when—"

"Last week?" Ice ran through her, freezing her sens
"You mean to tell me, you told Quinn last week."

"Mom, I… It just came out. I made him promise no
say anything, but he insisted I tell you if it hadn't gone av
in a week."

The ice turned to boiling heat. Quinn might have a g

heart, but he'd been undermining her parental rights. "He had no business making decisions for you again, Brandon. I'm telling you. This has to stop, or…"

The bottom fell out of her world. Or what? A war raged through her—head and heart, common sense and wisdom. She strode away, unable to discuss her confusion with him. "I'll talk with Quinn. You leave it alone."

"It's my life, Mom. Quinn's my friend and I thought yours. I'd think you'd be pleased I told an adult. One that I thought you respected. He's a man. So am I. Sometimes it's easier to talk with a man." He rose and stormed toward his bedroom. "But you just don't get it."

She glanced over her shoulder as he darted through the doorway. The slam of his bedroom door followed as she stood a moment to gather her wits. Instead of heading to the phone to tear into Quinn, she sailed through the dining room and slipped into a chair on the back porch.

A squirrel skittered past and climbed a tree while a chipmunk darted beneath a shrub. Hiding. Every being hid from what frightened them. She lifted her eyes to the bright blue sky, longing for the brightness to fill her and shine on the darkness she felt.

As her eyes closed, a prayer poured from her heart, a prayer for understanding, for patience, for letting go and giving her fears to the Lord. Quinn cared about them. That was a fact. He had wisdom, different from hers, but his ideas were sound. She had to release the tight control, the burden of fear and worry that she'd carried alone for the past years. If she didn't, her relationship with Quinn would end. Her chest ached with the anger that had burned inside her. She sat in silence broken only by the call of birds as the heat tempered and fell to ash.

Her thoughts turned to Brandon as another prayer rose for his health. God could do all things, and today trust had to be her pinion.

* * *

Quinn eyed the mantel clock as he paced the family ro
Ava's controlled voice still echoed in his ears, the mess
less angry than he anticipated. He wished he'd done thi
differently but he had no idea what that would be. W
Brandon spoke to him about the swelling, it was too la
ask him to tell, and how could he break the promise
made not to say anything to Ava? That was his mistake
shook his head. But then Brandon wouldn't have told h
Who knew how long the teen would have ignored the sy
tom?

No matter which way he turned he would never be ri
The problem hung like a cloud over their heads. If .
couldn't accept his involvement with her son, then how c(
anything come of their relationship? Though grateful that
hadn't gone berserk with Brandon's admission he had the
knowledge of the situation, Quinn knew the situation was
touchy.

Heavyhearted, he longed to call Ava's cell phone and
how the appointment had gone. He eyed his watch. T
might still be at the oncologist's office. Those things t
time. Even with prayer, remaining confident had becon
challenge.

His heart surged when he heard a sound at the door.
tap instead of the doorbell gave him assurance Brandon
arrived. He hurried to the door and opened it as Ava's
pulled away. Though confused, he kept his focus. "How
it go?"

He gave a one-shoulder shrug. "I'm scheduled for a
scan and biopsy on Friday. I won't know anything until th

"Dr. Franklin had no opinion?" He searched Brando
face.

"He couldn't offer an opinion from feeling the lymph n(
and he suspects it's not left from the mono. They'll take

node out and check the area for abnormalities." He shook his head. "I've been through this before."

Quinn slipped his arm around the teen's shoulder and gave him a squeeze. "I'll keep praying, okay?" He patted his back and lowered his arm. "Hungry or do you want to drive?"

"Drive." A faint grin curved his mouth. "Driving's the best thing I'll do today."

Quinn grinned back but his heart wasn't in it. "Don't you think seeing the oncologist was the best? Wait and see." He prayed he was right. "How's your mom? I thought she'd stop, too."

"She's okay. She has an appointment to look at the house of that lady who came here the other day."

"Megan?"

He nodded. "She wants Mom to decorate her house." His face brightened. "I didn't know my mom had a talent like that. She always did things around our house, but…" He shrugged. "I guess when it's in your face you don't recognize it."

The truth of his statement hit him. Ava and Bran had slipped into his heart in a way he didn't recognize at first. He called it helping, being generous, caring, everything but what it was. He'd grown to love them both. Time didn't matter. Months or years meant nothing where real God-given love was involved.

He reached in his pocket for the car keys and tossed them to Brandon. "I thought your mom would be more angry when she learned I knew about the swelling first."

"She was at first. I saw it in her face, but later, she must have thought about it or something. She hasn't said anymore about it."

Quinn let the information soak in, hoping to sort it out and understand what her change of heart meant. It was a good sign. "Ready?"

Brandon led the way, his enthusiasm evident, and seeing

him with something else on his mind besides his latest health
scare lifted Quinn's spirit. Hoping on this trip he could leave
stress behind, he opened the passenger door and eased in. The
teen's experience behind the wheel showed his driving skill.
He'd learned well.

"Where to?" Bran slipped the key into the ignition.

"Freeway again? Let's drive out Woodward and pick it up
at Square Lake."

Bran agreed, and Quinn clamped his mouth closed, wanting to control his comments. Traffic picked up on Woodward as they approached Square Lake Road. Four-thirty
meant jammed traffic as people headed home from work.
Bad timing. Brandon followed the signs to I-75, maneuvering
his way onto the freeway as lanes vanished and cars fought
for space on the road.

Quinn held his breath, then let it go when Brandon had
managed to guide his SUV into an open lane. "Good job."
He managed to maintain silence until the sign for Sashabaw
Road appeared and he made a decision. "Let's head back.
The traffic is only going to get worse."

Brandon nodded again, his focus on the traffic, and made
his way into the exit lane. He pulled from the freeway, turned
left and followed the signs to reenter I-75 heading south.
Though he impressed Quinn with his skills, the old memories prickled his spine. Driving at this time of day had been
a poor idea.

Moving along with traffic, Quinn relaxed. Brandon stayed
close to the right lane, ready for an exit a few miles up the
road. A car in the next lane, hovering ahead of them, drove
too slow for the freeway traffic, and he noted cars maneuvering past. Too slow seemed as bad as too fast. A white
car charged behind the slow-moving car, blew his horn and
veered onto their lane, cutting off the SUV, but Bran braked
in time, and the car sped on.

Brandon released a stream of air. "Wow. That was stupid."

"You did very well. Drivers always have to be on their toes." Enough.

A squeal ripped through the traffic ahead of them. The white car zigzagged across a lane and spun out of control, sending two cars flying.

The second car headed toward their lane, and Quinn braced himself. Brakes squealed as cars swerved out of the way, but another slid toward them. Quinn's heart rose to his throat and he reached to grab the wheel, but Brandon veered away and shot to the right into the shoulder as the car behind him barreled into the fray. The screech of brakes and crunch of metal resounded around them.

Brandon stepped on the brake and skidded to a stop. Cars bunched beside them, some damaged, some unscathed, having avoided the accident as they did. Quinn gaped at the mayhem that Brandon had avoided. He wanted to embrace the boy. Instead he uttered his gratefulness for his quick thinking, and they sat without speaking, listening to the sound of sirens in the distance.

Quinn's mind raced back to his years of guilt, dealing with the notion that he could have stopped Sean's accident from happening. Today, reality took over. Brandon's skill and God's blessing saved them from the crash. Quinn acknowledged his hand on the wheel could have caused a disaster. Instead Bran had used the skill he'd learned.

Quinn's angst washed away. Ava had lectured him weeks earlier, and she had been right. Though he still didn't comprehend, Sean's and Lydia's deaths had a purpose. From the tragedy, he'd altered his priorities and values. He'd become a better man.

And now the life he'd come to know filled a void he'd lived with for years. He'd been a believer but not a listener. God's commandments and desires had taken second place to his own wants. Not anymore. He'd grown closer to the Lord. He changed his life from taking to giving, and with Ava's influ-

ence, he'd honed a new life, one he would never have anticipated years earlier.

Quinn looked at his watch. "We'll be stuck here awhile,
I'm afraid. We'd better call your mom so she's not worried."

Brandon agreed, his focus on the havoc around them, his
hands trembling on the wheel.

He pressed his palm on the boy's shoulder and squeezed
it, hoping the love he felt reached the teen's heart. Brandon
looked at him with tears brimming on the edge of his eyes.

"Thanks." He twisted sideways and wrapped his arm
around Quinn's shoulder. They sat there in silence.

Chapter Sixteen

Ava rested her hand on Brandon's, her eyes focusing on the needle taped against his arm. She followed the plastic tubing to the IV bag hanging above his head. How many times had she faced this same situation? Earlier they'd performed the CT scan that could detect abnormalities in his chest, neck, abdomen and pelvic areas. She prayed the test discovered nothing.

Dr. Franklin had spent time with them reviewing why he had chosen an open biopsy rather than the procedure that used only a needle to remove a sample of the node for testing. With Brandon's Hodgkin's struggle, the open biopsy would remove the node and allow the surgeon to examine the surrounding areas. Though a more invasive procedure, Ava agreed it would be the most revealing, providing them with the most accurate diagnosis.

Bran's heavy eyes opened then closed. She didn't break the silence. She'd spoken to the surgeon, and when he left, she knew she could expect the surgical technicians to arrive soon to transport him to the surgical area. The procedure wasn't new. Brandon's biopsies had become commonplace, and the worry wasn't new, either.

The triage curtain slid open, and two young men stepped

inside. Her time with Brandon had ended, and now the waiting began. She'd experienced the trip to the waiting room numerous times before. When she leaned down and kissed Brandon's cheek, he mumbled something she didn't catch, but she tucked it in her heart anyway.

Her shoes clicked on the tile as she made her way to the waiting area. She settled into a chair near the door and searched through the magazines piled on the table beside her. *Homes and Gardens* caught her eye, but as her fingers turned the pages, her mind stepped away.

The accident Quinn and Brandon narrowly escaped replayed in her head many times since the past Tuesday. When they'd arrived home and she heard the details of what had happened, she sent up a prayer of thanksgiving, and she told Bran how proud she was of him. She'd feared his learning to drive, but Quinn attested that he was a capable driver who'd learned well. Her gratefulness multiplied.

Though rejoicing, she recalled the impact the accident had on Quinn. When they were alone, he admitted that she'd been correct all along. He could have done nothing to divert Sean's accident. Seeing his face as he talked assured her that the heavy guilt he'd carried would diminish in time. The awareness was raw.

Now her challenge was to rid herself of the flaw that could ruin their relationship. She'd avoided talking about Quinn's previous knowledge of Bran's lymph node. When she considered the facts, she faced how much Quinn had impacted their lives. Bran related to Quinn as a father. The bond they'd formed outshone her ridiculous envy. It was what she wanted for her son—a man to help him through his teen years, to teach him to be a good father and husband, and to steer his walk with the Lord.

Though she would never be perfect, Ava hoped to monitor the begrudging attitude she displayed to Quinn. Many times, Brandon would feel more comfortable talking to a man about his concerns. He'd indicated that the day he admitted the swelling.

So why had she discouraged Quinn from being with her today? The decision had caused her regret. All day, she'd longed for his company and support. Instead of behaving as she should, she'd allowed her self-importance to control her decision. She pressed her shoulders against the seat to relieve the tension and opened the magazine. An article on renovating a home on a budget captured her attention. Megan had expressed interest in her doing the job the day she'd visited her home, and the article offered great inexpensive decorating tips. Megan's house screamed with potential.

With the accident the center of their conversation the last time she saw Quinn, she hadn't told him about her visit with Megan. She looked forward to sharing the news. The idea to take the job, though exciting, challenged her. Decorating Quinn's home had opened a door for her, but she'd felt more confident than she did now. She wished she'd had more training than reading magazines, watching design shows on TV, and having God-given talent others had expressed. Another trust issue bunched in her head. Trust God for with Him all things were possible.

As she delved back into the magazine, ideas popped into her mind. If only…

A shadow fell across her page, and without looking, she knew Quinn stood above her. She lifted her gaze while her pulse skipped like a child at play. "You must have read my thoughts."

What had been a serious expression brightened. "I wish I had, Ava. I just took my chances, but I couldn't stay away. Brandon means—"

She grasped his hand. "I know. He's the next best thing to a son."

Tears brimmed on the rim of his eyes and melted Ava's heart. The man who'd hidden his emotions for years allowed his feelings to emerge. She rose and wrapped her arms around him. "I've been a jerk, Quinn. I've hurt you by trying to maintain my own importance in Bran's life, and it's—"

He held her close and pressed his finger to her lips. "You'll always be important to Brandon. You've said it yourself a million times. You're his mother. Mother's are pivotal in their children's lives. I don't know why you ever doubted that."

"I don't, either." She sank back into the chair, probing her mind for reasons.

Quinn lifted the magazine she'd dropped on the chair beside her and sat. "Any news yet?"

She shook her head. "He had the CT scan earlier, and they're doing the biopsy now. I don't know if they'll keep him or send him home today."

"I guess we wait and see." He eyed the magazine he'd lifted from the chair. "Good reading?"

Grateful for the distraction, she took it from his hands. "Perfect." His question was perfect, too, opening the door for her visit with Megan. She related what happened during her visit, explained the article and admitted her fears. "Can I do this? If so, do I want to?"

He searched her eyes. "Is that even a question?"

Quinn understood her well. "Not really. I'd love to take on the job. It's exciting and creative. And it gives me an opportunity to explore my ability." She placed her hand on his. "Remember when I told you that Bran once said I didn't have a life and that I was living his?"

His face acknowledged his recollection.

"That wouldn't be true anymore. I have a life now, and though he'll always be a focus, I've learned I can be multifaceted. Bran and design..." Her pulse clipped along faster than it had been. "And you."

He covered her hand and squeezed. "I hope you mean that."

"I do. From the bottom of my heart."

Quinn's eyelids grew heavy, and she read the longing on his face. He wanted to kiss her, and she wanted to kiss him back, but a hospital waiting room wasn't the appropriate setting. Instead, he slipped his arm around her and nestled her shoulder against his. They faded into silence, her thoughts on Brandon and the happiness she found in Quinn.

"Ava, have you ever considered—"

"Mrs. Darnell."

Though Quinn's question intrigued her, the surgeon's voice captured her attention. She rose and hurried to the doorway. When she realized Quinn had stayed behind, she beckoned him to follow. He looked at her with question so she gestured again, and he rose.

In the hallway, her heart pounded as she searched Dr. Franklin's face. "Is he—"

"Brandon's in recovery. He's fine, and once I take a final look at him, I think he can go home with you, but it may be a while."

"Results?" She knew the answer but the question had to be asked.

He gave one turn of his head. "You know I can't have results this soon. Everything looked fine, but the biopsy and CT scan will let us know for sure."

Her mouth opened to ask her next question.

"I've asked them to hurry on the results. No promises, but I hope to let you know before the end of next week."

She'd experienced the wait before. "Thank you, Dr. Franklin."

He shook her hand. "A nurse will let you know when you can see him." He strode away, leaving a void in her chest.

Focusing on Quinn, she released a sigh. "The wait will seem like forever."

He nodded and slipped her hand into his. "Be grateful he asked for a rush on the results."

Ava needed Quinn's positive approach. When they re-seated, Quinn's last question returned. "Have I ever considered what?" Her chest constricted as he heart flew to possibilities.

"Have you considered going into a real business?"

The question bogged her mind. "You mean—"

He chuckled. "Hanging out your shingle."

"You mean advertising that I'm a designer?"

His expression answered her question as he wove her fingers though his. "You'd start small. Business cards, a portfolio of the work you've done. You'd need before-and-after photos on this job. It would only take a little seed money to get started."

"I can barely afford birdseed let alone money for a business."

Though he chuckled, his expression showed his disappointment in her.

"I'm glad you think it's funny, Quinn, but—"

"I would invest, Ava. The amount is trivial, and if you want to be sole owner, you could pay me back on your first job."

Excitement bloomed on his face as doom but she couldn't overcome her own doubts. "I love the work, Quinn, but I'm not trained. I don't have any credentials to prove I'm qualified for real business. Who'd want to hire someone like me?"

"Megan." He sent her a coy grin. "And me." He searched her face. "And I'll never be sorry…for many reasons."

The innuendo didn't escape her.

"Why not take some classes? Check out Oakland Community College. It's right here in Royal Oak, or what about online classes? You'd end up with some training and a portfolio, too." She opened her mouth, but he raised his palm and continued. "I know that would take time, but you'd still have opportunities with people who learn about your work. Look at what happened with Megan. And once you have a few classes under you belt, you can start promoting the business."

"Short- and long-range planning." She looked into his eyes, recognizing his sincerity.

"That's how a business succeeds. You need both."

Her mind spun with his encouragement and her doubt. "You're overwhelming me. I need time to think." Her greatest concern centered in her mind. "And I can't make any decisions until I know how Brandon is. If this is Hodgkin's then—"

His excitement diminished, and he lowered his head. "That's the most important." When Quinn looked up, he gestured to the doorway.

A nurse stood in the threshold, scanning those waiting. In a moment, Ava heard her name. She gave Quinn a look to follow her and rose. Instead of an argument, he walked beside her down the hallway, as she sent up a prayer for Brandon's good report. He'd roused and could go home.

Looking forward to the firework display, Quinn toted a cooler while Brandon lugged three lawn chairs and a blanket into Clawson City Park. Different from many cities who held their holiday fireworks days earlier, Clawson held their event on July Fourth.

Pleased that his relationship with Ava had smoothed and grown, his hope remained that one day they could make a commitment, but in the same way Bran's cancer held Ava back from considering her own business, he knew making any kind of commitment with him would be held at bay. When he proposed, he wanted a wholehearted yes.

One issue still dragged on his mind. His relationship with Dreams Come True Foundation. He'd avoided talking about it, and he'd also taken another step without Ava's approval that could dredge up trouble. Tonight he needed to talk about it.

"Is this okay?"

Ava's voice stopped his thoughts. He eyed the tree behind them. "I think so. The tree doesn't block our view. What do you think, Bran?"

The boy leaned the three chairs against the tree trunk and shrugged. "Fine, I guess."

Quinn studied his face as he set the cooler beside the chairs. As Ava spread the blanket, he slipped beside Brandon. "Talk to me."

Surprise lit Brandon face, but, in a flash, turned to question. "What do you mean?"

"You know what I mean. Something's on your mind."

Brandon shrugged again. "Some of my friends are here, and I'd like to hang with them."

"Why can't you?" He searched the boy's face.

He gave Quinn an are-you-stupid look and flicked his shoulder toward his mother. "She'll be upset."

Quinn reviewed the possibilities. "Why?"

"She's worried about the lymph node so she's the gestapo again."

He hoped Brandon was wrong. "Ask her."

Brandon pressed his lips together, studying Quinn's face. "Are you sure?"

Quinn nodded.

"Mom."

Ava looked up. "What?"

At first he hesitated but garnered his courage. "Some of my buddies are here, and I want to hang out with them. Is that okay?"

Her eyes flashed to Quinn, her concern evident.

Quinn held his breath as he watched her struggle.

"Can you find them and then let us know where you are?"

Brandon gave a nod, surprise written on his face. "I'll be back."

As he hurried away, Quinn grinned at Ava and held out

his hand. She grasped it, and he drew her as close as he was comfortable in a public place. "Thanks. I know that wasn't easy."

"No, but it was right."

The desire to kiss her overwhelmed him. Instead, he gave her a squeeze and went about unfolding the chairs and pulling two cans of pop from the cooler. He flipped the tabs and handed one to Ava. She took a sip and sat in one of the chairs, studying the sky where they would observe the holiday display.

Quinn took a drink from the can before he settled beside her. Dusk had fallen, and he wanted to get the discussion out in the open before the fireworks. He eyed his watch. Nine. They had an hour, he suspected. After another drink, he set the can near his feet and rested his hand on hers. "I was proud of your response to Brandon."

"I know what's best to do, but part of me fights it." She shook her head as she spoke.

"That's what makes me proud." He gathered the words he'd rehearsed in his mind. "Ava, since we're talking about Brandon, I—"

"Hey!"

His head snapped up as Lexie strode toward them. "We were checking on the kids, and Ethan spotted you."

Ava rose and strode to her. "Kids?"

Lexie gave Ava a hug. "Kelsey and Ross are here, too, with the girls. They're with Cooper goofing around at the playground. It's been a crazy day. We went to the Clawson parade this morning. The kids loved it, and here we are for the finale." She motioned beyond the playground. "Want to join us? We're right over there."

Ava gave Quinn a questioning look, but he shook his head. "Brandon is hanging out with friends and he'd never find us in this crowd if we moved, but thanks for the invitation."

"Next year we'll have to make plans." Lexie took a step

back. "It's getting darker. We'd better get back." She gave
wave and hurried off.

Ava turned around, and he beckoned her to sit, anxious
get back to the conversation. "To be honest, I like both co
ples, but it's kind of nice being alone."

Her sweet smile wove around his heart. "It is." She a
justed the chair and sat. "Anyway you'd just said somethi
about Brandon."

He regrouped. "I did." He sank into the chair beside h
"His birthday is in two days, right?"

"Yes, July sixth."

He'd worked on this script since he'd acted on a whim. I
pressed his lips together and decided to get it out. "I want
to give him something special for his birthday. He'll be si
teen, and I'm praying we'll be celebrating a clean bill
health."

"We're both praying for that, and hopefully we'll he
something soon." Her gaze shifted for a moment as she m
tioned in the direction Lexie had retreated. "Lexie's a
Kelsey's family have been blessed. All three kids are doi
so well. Peyton's meds are controlling her cardiomyopath
Cooper's leukemia has been in remission so long, and Lu
hasn't had a brain tumor for over two years." She lower
her gaze. "I'm ashamed, Quinn, when sometimes I wond
how many blessings the Lord has to hand out."

Quinn's chest tightened, and he kissed her fingers. "Y
know blessings aren't limited, because God's not limite
Pray with confidence." He caught her gaze. "You have to.

"I know." She lifted her shoulders and sighed.

Silence covered them, and he looked up noticing stars h
begun to show in the sky. Soon the stars would be oversha
owed by the fireworks. As he scanned the crowd, he sp
ted Brandon maneuvering through the blankets and chai
Quinn pointed, and Ava waved.

"I'm straight ahead, Mom." Brandon pointed beyond t

playground to the crowd ahead. "I'll come back here when it's over."

She agreed, and Brandon hurried back the way he'd come.

Ava watched a moment, then shifted her attention back to him. "Did you want me to give you gift ideas for Bran?"

The question unloosed his reservations. "I know what I want to give him."

"You do?" Her eyes captured his. "What?"

"A car."

Her jaw dropped as she pulled in air. "But we talked about that, and I said—"

He placed his finger across her lips. "Shh, and listen."

She closed her mouth, but the dazed look remained.

"When you refused my offer, you thought I was involved in some kind of scheme."

"Quinn, I—"

"My turn." He arched a brow, and she swallowed her words. "You had no idea how much money I had, and though you still don't know numbers, you know that I own a successful corporation that gives me great financial rewards, and you know that I believe in sharing what the Lord has given me."

She nodded.

"Brandon is like a son to me. You know that."

She nodded again.

"I would like your permission to give him a car. It's used, but in excellent condition. It's the one Randy told me about."

"But that was weeks ago." A frown glided across her face. "Are you sure no one has bought it already?"

"Someone has." She looked confused, and he couldn't help but laugh. "I bought the car when Randy told me about it."

"You did?"

"I did." He slid from the chair to the blanket and patted the ground. "Come sit with me."

"You thought you'd change my mind." She rose and eased onto the cover beside him.

"I hoped." He wrapped his arm around her and drew her close, nestling her against his shoulder. "Giving is a joy to me, Ava."

"You've given us too much." She covered his hand with hers.

"And you've given me as much, but before the fireworks begin, I have one more thing to tell you." He felt her body tense. "You asked me a few weeks ago if I'd every heard of the Dreams Come True Foundation."

"You said yes."

"But I didn't tell you everything." Surprising him, Ava pressed her index finger over his lips.

"You don't have to. I've known for a while now."

"Known?" This time he'd tensed. "But how did you—"

"I've come to know you, Quinn, and I began to understand your love of giving. One day when you were in Grand Rapids, I noticed a letter from your lawyer in the stack of mail I pulled off your desk when I spilled the water. The words *Dreams Come True Foundation* jumped out at me." She caught his gaze. "I didn't read the letter. I felt guilty having seen that much. So I began to suspect…"

As he listened to her explanation, his heart soared. She'd figured it out on her own and hadn't said a word.

"What hurt me—" she gazed into his eyes "—was that you didn't trust me enough to tell me. You thought I'd tell everyone, and I hope you—"

"I know you wouldn't now, Ava, but you have so many friends who know about the foundation and I knew it might be difficult not to slip." His excuse sounded feeble, but it was true. "It sounds feeble now, but I need the donor to be anonymous. The importance shouldn't be on the giver. I don't want thanks. God is the giver, and He deserves the thanks." He cupped her cheek in his palm. "I wanted to tell you the truth, Ava, but I misjudged you. I don't want any secrets between us."

"I'm an open book."

"Finally, I am, too." The years he'd spent boxed in with all his guilt and secrets were gone. He gazed into her smiling eyes, and in the cover of darkness, he lowered his lips to hers, enjoying the feel of her body next to his, her heart beating with his as one. His pulse raced as his yearning grew to tell her what was in his heart. He deepened the kiss as a sizzle split the air followed by a reverberating blast.

He drew back in time to see a splay of red, white and blue shimmering through the sky, the glow lighting Ava's lovely face. She looked at him with heavy eyes. "I thought the explosion was my heart."

He laughed as he drew her into his arms again.

Chapter Seventeen

Ava stood over the sink, rinsing the dishes from Brand[...] birthday party dinner. With the surprise birthday gift i[...] garage, Quinn had asked her to have the party at his ho[...] It worked for the best since the party consisted of Br[...] buddies along with Quinn and her, and the teens enjc[...] the yard.

The telephone call she'd received that morning hugge[...] heart. Their prayers had been answered. An appointmen[...] the following week would provide details, but on the ph[...] Dr. Franklin relayed Brandon's CT scan and biopsy sho[...] no signs of Hodgkin's. The swollen gland resulted from [...] lier treatment and had been aggravated by the mononuc[...] sis. The words sang in her head. *Cancer-free.*

The sound of the basketball striking the backboard an[...] teens' laughter rang in her ears. She leaned her back ag[...] the sink, enjoying the amazing sound. A year ago her [...] tude had landed her in the doldrums. Instead of looking [...] the positive, as the devil's advocate that she had become[...] looked for both—positive and negative, then leaned tov[...] the latter. Defeat had filled her since Tom's death.

Life had proved difficult with Brandon's health and t[...] financial struggles. Tom's sudden death had ripped a ho[...]

her dreams and hopes. God lived on the outskirts of her life, near but not present. A prayer rose from her heart, thanking Him for all He'd done. If she had it all to do over, she would have backed into Quinn on purpose. She chuckled at the thought.

"What's the joke?"

Quinn's voice revived her from her musing. Her pulse skipped as it still did each time she saw him. "Thinking of you."

He ambled across the room and took her in his arms. "I hope all the time."

His lips touched hers while her heart pounded in her chest. When he drew back, she lifted her eyes to his. "I don't have words." She cupped his face in her hands. "When I met you, my dreams had died. My one hope was for Brandon's health, and though the wonderful news came this morning, it's still my biggest hope. But for once, I now have dreams, too."

"You know I want to make dreams happen, Ava." He lifted her hand to his lips and kissed her fingers. "I pray you'll let me."

His prayer filtered in Ava's thoughts. "You've been amazing to us. Amazing." The need to be open pressed on her mind. "But the longings I have now can't be purchased with money."

"Then how about with love?"

The look in his eyes sent her reeling. Love. She had only hoped. Today she'd heard the words she'd hoped for. She studied his face. "You mean that?"

Quinn meant it with every beat of his heart. "Oh, Ava. I've loved you forever it seems. Before you, my world had been empty and guilt-ridden." He gestured toward the joyful sounds from the backyard. "And look at it now." His lips touched hers again, deep and certain.

He drew back and reached into his pocket. "I know this is Brandon's birthday, but it's a day to remember. Cancer-free.

His sixteenth year." His eyes captured hers. "I've neve[r]
a dream of my own, either, but I have since meeting yo[u]
drew his hand from his pocket. "And today my own d[ream]
will come true, if you say yes."

Ava's eyes widened, and her hand clutched at her c[...]
He gazed at the Claddagh pendant she seemed to wear [...]
day, knowing that every symbol told the truth about hi[s...]
for her.

He opened the velvet box and withdrew the diamond[.]
Prisms of light shot from the princess cut with smalle[r dia]
monds embedding the gold band. He placed the ring i[n her]
hand, her face radiant as she studied the nuances of the s[...]

Surprise lit her face. "Is the diamond pink? It's mag[nifi]
cent."

With the ring in Ava's hand, his dream surrounde[d and]
embraced him. He drew in air, his lungs as full as his h[...]
"A tinge of pink. It's unique like you."

Her eyes searched his. "Quinn, I'd love you to put it o[n my]
finger."

He soared on clouds. "Does that mean yes?"

She wrapped her arms around his neck, offering her [...]
That was all the answer he needed to know that his d[ream]
had come true.

With the ring on her finger, they walked outside tog[ether,]
and when Brandon looked up, he grinned at the boy. "[...]
a minute?"

He bounced the ball to Mike and met him on the p[...]
"Thanks for the great party."

"You're always welcome." He motioned to Ava. "[...]
mom has something to tell you."

Before he moved, Brandon's eyes lowered to her h[...]
His grin opened to a smile, and he raised his hand in a h[igh]
five. "I've been waiting for this." He threw his arms ar[ound]
Quinn's neck and then ran to Ava and swung her aroun[d]

When he set her on her feet again, tears filled her eyes. "God has been good to us, Bran."

He kissed her cheek. "I'm happier than I've been in years, Mom." He spun around. "Hey guys, look at this." He lifted her hand and pointed to the ring.

The boys surrounded them with congratulations on their lips, and when they calmed, Quinn caught Brandon's attention. "Do me a favor. In the excitement, I forgot to get your birthday gift out of the garage."

Curiosity filled Brandon's face. He didn't hesitate but dashed toward the garage door. As he neared, Quinn hit the door opener on his key chain. As the door opened, Brandon came to a ragged stop, almost falling over himself. He eyed Quinn, realization filling his face. "You're kidding."

"No joke. It's yours."

By then his friends spotted the car, a 2008 bright red sport sedan in perfect condition. Yells and yahoos filled the yard, and while they were occupied inside the garage, he drew Ava in his arms. Without a word, his lips lowered to hers, and he drank in the glorious sense of wholeness. She'd opened his eyes and his world, and he was ready to live again.

June the following year

Ava stood outside on the sidewalk, admiring the colorful buildings lining the main street of downtown Dingle, Ireland—pastel green, pink, soft yellow and fieldstone—advertising their businesses with signs that read Murphy's Pub, Sheehy's Supermarket and Ashe's Seafood. Since arriving in Ireland, she'd seen many sites that opened her eyes to a world she had never known. The country spread out in a blanket of green, every shade she could imagine, dotted with lovely cottages, dry stone fences and sheep, their wooly coats sprayed with colorful markings to identify them.

Earlier in the day they'd followed the Ring of Kerry, view-

ing the small villages filled with friendly people. Quin
talked about his family, and as they planned their h
moon, she felt as if she knew them. Once she'd met
they were all he had promised and more.

Brandon's good health report added to the joy of the
When they arrived, he'd been surrounded by Quinn's
age cousins who yearned for stories about the United
as much as she and Brandon longed to learn more abou
land. Bran even brought along his own camera to reco
amazing trip Quinn had planned for them. He called it
Family's Dream Come True."

And it had been. In May, their quiet wedding with
family and a few friends fulfilled their earlier commit
With God working His astounding plan, she and Quin
bumped into each other at the hardware store, and lif
never been the same. Plans for her home design career
in the making. Following her work on Megan's house,
applied for home design classes at Oakland Community
lege in the fall, but without any credentials, she alread
three word-of-mouth jobs from friends of friends. An
way the Lord worked in her life.

Quinn stepped through the market door, tucking his
in his pocket. "We need to be on our way."

He opened a bottle of water and handed it to her. She
a long drink, admiring her new husband. "I'm sorry Br
opted out of this trip today. It's been amazing."

"He's having fun with the cousins, and we'll meet up
him for dinner. We're driving to Slea Head and the fa
will be waiting for us at Stone House Restaurant. The
ing is a long stretch of fieldstone topped by a thatche
overlooking miles of the Atlantic Ocean. So if we hur
He chucked her under the chin. "We'll see the sunset b
dinner." He wove his fingers with hers and ambled to th
he'd rented when they arrived.

"I can't wait." She squeezed his hand as he let go to

her door, and inside the car she leaned back, pinching herself that she had been walking the streets of Ireland for nearly a week. By now, she understood Quinn's reference to hurrying. Between driving on narrow hedgerow-lined lanes and roads blocked by herds of sheep, trips always took longer than expected.

Her thoughts slipped back to their visit to Tralee, Adare and Killarney, towns she'd heard about from old songs her grandmother sometimes sang. Brandon's excitement added to her memories. The overwhelming experience stretched her mind and fostered greater dreams of traveling places she'd never been.

"You're quiet."

Putting her thoughts on hold, she smiled at Quinn. "I'm thinking about this amazing trip, an experience of a lifetime."

"This is only the first, Ava. You name the place, and we can go." He patted her leg and the warmth of his palm settled in her heart.

"You've married a simple woman with few experiences."

"Just the kind of woman I love. We can see God's world together."

Her eyes misted as her old troubles washed away, yet Quinn made their joys guilt-free. He continued to fund Dreams Come True, and now that they were married, she watched him write check after check for charities at home and around the world. It was his joy.

Quinn had once quoted the scripture that guided his life. *Do not store up for yourselves treasures on earth, where moth and rust destroy, and where thieves break in and steal. But store up for yourselves treasures in heaven.* It now guided hers.

Ava gazed across the landscape, watching the sun lower in the sky and touching the distant hills. Her stomach made a soft growl. Hours had passed since they'd eaten, but the wait was worth it. As Quinn slowed, she looked out across the stretch of water that rolled to the rocky cliffs. Already the setting sun had tipped the clouds with coral and purple. Gold and burnished orange painted the ragged shoreline and white-topped waves rolled into the umber rocks below.

Quinn stepped out, rounded the car and opened her door. When she stood beside him, he drew her closer to the edge of the cliffs where the sound of surf lashed the rocks below. In the ebb and surge, she almost heard an Irish melody. Quinn slipped his arm around her shoulders, his touch thrilling her even more than it had months ago at her first inkling of romance.

Ava sighed, and he turned pressing her to his body, kissing her nose and eyes before covering her lips with his. When the kiss ended, Quinn buried his face in her neck, his words of love greeting her ear. She would never tire of his affection. Her eyes searched the distant golden-tipped ocean, taking her breath away, but never as fully as Quinn's love and kisses. A prayer of thanks to the Lord rippled on her heart, and her praise rose heavenward where hopes and dreams came true.

* * * * *

Dear Reader,

You've come to the end of the Dreams Come True series, and I hope you've enjoyed all of the stories. Though the characters' lives were filled with challenge, God stood by their sides, providing them with what they needed to stay strong and marriage partners to provide them with joy and love.

I hope while you were entertained by these stories, you were also strengthened by God's Word and His love. We are never alone in our trials, and though sometimes we grow frustrated or doubting, we find our way back to His arms where He holds us close and provides us with strength, courage and faith.

Each story stressed different aspects of the families' struggles, but in every story, trust and hope seemed paramount. With God by our sides, we have no need to doubt. Trust in Him and in Him we have hope. By visiting my website at www.gailmartin.com, you can subscribe to my online newsletter and keep up with my books and appearances, recipes and a monthly devotional. Please look for my next release.

Wishing you blessings always.

Gail Gaymer Martin

Questions for Discussion

1. Ava and Quinn met in the hardware store parking lot in a fender-bender. Both blamed the other person. Who did you blame? Were you correct? How did you make that decision?

2. Most people bring flaws and concerns into new relationships. What did you see as Ava's biggest flaw? Quinn's biggest flaw? Do you have flaws that sometimes affect your relationships?

3. What qualities did you identify in Ava and Quinn that made them interesting characters?

4. Have you dealt with a loss in your personal life? Ava and Quinn both lost their spouses, and Quinn lost his only child, too. How did their losses affect their lives? How did you make it through your loss or losses?

5. Has a child in your life experienced a severe illness? How did you cope with the stress? What gave you strength?

6. Have you been involved in a support group such as the one in the three stories? Were you comfortable sharing your problems and fears? In what way do these groups provide support for members?

7. Ava was a talker and resented people who are closed-mouthed like Quinn. Have you met someone who has an attribute so different from yours it frustrated you?

8. Did Brandon seem like a typical teenager? In what way? What were Brandon's good qualities? Could you understand Brandon's resentment with his mother?

9. Ava's struggle to let go of her control affected both her and Brandon. If you had been in Ava's shoes, how might you have handled her problems and worries about Brandon?

10. Ava had an unused God-given talent that Quinn helped her experience. Do you have a talent that you wish you could have developed? Is it possible for you to use it now?

11. Quinn led a life of wealth and success, yet realized after his tragedy that those goals were no longer satisfying. What was Quinn missing in life? What made him change?

12. Did you agree with Quinn's need to remain anonymous as donor of Dreams Come True Foundation? Were you surprised when you learned the secret everyone in the three novels wanted to know? When were you certain that Quinn was the donor?

13. If you were wealthy enough to support a foundation, what type of organization would it fund and why?

14. What was your favorite part of the story and why?

INSPIRATIONAL

Love Inspired®

celebrating 15 YEARS

COMING NEXT MONTH
AVAILABLE JUNE 19, 2012

MONTANA COWBOY
The McKaslin Clan
Jillian Hart
Montana cowboy Luke McKaslin hits it off with Honor Crosby on a book lovers' website, but will the wealthy city girl fit into his humble small-town life?

HER SURPRISE SISTER
Texas Twins
Marta Perry
If the discovery of a twin sister isn't shocking enough for Violet Colby, imagine her surprise when she finds herself falling for Landon Derringer—her twin's former fiancé!

WILDFLOWER BRIDE IN DRY CREEK
Return to Dry Creek
Janet Tronstad
Security expert Tyler Stone was hired to find runaway heiress Angelina Brighton, but will this assignment turn into a matter of the heart?

THE DOCTOR'S DEVOTION
Eagle Point Emergency
Cheryl Wyatt
When former combat surgeon Mitch Wellington and nurse Lauren Bates find themselves working side by side at a trauma center, they learn that love is the best medicine.

A FAMILY TO CHERISH
Men of Allegany County
Ruth Logan Herne
Former high school sweethearts Cam Calhoun and Meredith Brennan find themselves working on a project together—can they move beyond the past and possibly find a future?

AND FATHER MAKES THREE
Kim Watters
Desperate for a cure for her adopted daughter's leukemia, Elizabeth Randall contacts her daughter's biological father—could Blake Crawford be a match in more ways than one?

Look for these and other Love Inspired books wherever books are sold, including most bookstores, supermarkets, discount stores and drugstores.

LICNM0612

REQUEST YOUR FREE BOOKS!

2 FREE INSPIRATIONAL NOVELS
PLUS 2
FREE
MYSTERY GIFTS

Love Inspired

YES! Please send me 2 FREE Love Inspired® novels and my 2 FREE mystery gifts (gifts are worth about $10). After receiving them, if I don't wish to receive any more books, I can return the shipping statement marked "cancel." If I don't cancel, I will receive 6 brand-new novels every month and be billed just $4.49 per book in the U.S. or $4.99 per book in Canada. That's a saving of at least 22% off the cover price. It's quite a bargain! Shipping and handling is just 50¢ per book in the U.S. and 75¢ per book in Canada.* I understand that accepting the 2 free books and gifts places me under no obligation to buy anything. I can always return a shipment and cancel at any time. Even if I never buy another book, the two free books and gifts are mine to keep forever.

105/305 IDN FEGR

Name _____ (PLEASE PRINT) _____

Address _____ Apt. # _____

City _____ State/Prov. _____ Zip/Postal Code _____

Signature (if under 18, a parent or guardian must sign)

Mail to the **Reader Service:**
IN U.S.A.: P.O. Box 1867, Buffalo, NY 14240-1867
IN CANADA: P.O. Box 609, Fort Erie, Ontario L2A 5X3

Not valid for current subscribers to Love Inspired books.

**Are you a subscriber to Love Inspired books
and want to receive the larger-print edition?
Call 1-800-873-8635 or visit www.ReaderService.com.**

* Terms and prices subject to change without notice. Prices do not include applicable taxes. Sales tax applicable in N.Y. Canadian residents will be charged applicable taxes. Offer not valid in Quebec. This offer is limited to one order per household. All orders subject to credit approval. Credit or debit balances in a customer's account(s) may be offset by any other outstanding balance owed by or to the customer. Please allow 4 to 6 weeks for delivery. Offer available while quantities last.

Your Privacy—The Reader Service is committed to protecting your privacy. Our Privacy Policy is available online at www.ReaderService.com or upon request from the Reader Service.

We make a portion of our mailing list available to reputable third parties that offer products we believe may interest you. If you prefer that we not exchange your name with third parties, or if you wish to clarify or modify your communication preferences, please visit us at www.ReaderService.com/consumerschoice or write to us at Reader Service Preference Service, P.O. Box 9062, Buffalo, NY 14269. Include your complete name and address.

LIREG11B

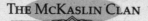

Fairy tales do come true with fan-favorite author

Jillian Hart

Honor Crosby never thought she would find a man she
could trust again, especially not in an online book group.
But when Honor finds herself heading to Luke McKaslin's
Montana ranch to see if their chemistry works offline,
her fantasy becomes too real. Can Honor believe in love…
even as she falls for Luke?

Montana Cowboy

The McKaslin Clan

*Available July
wherever books are sold.*

www.LoveInspiredBooks.com

LI87751